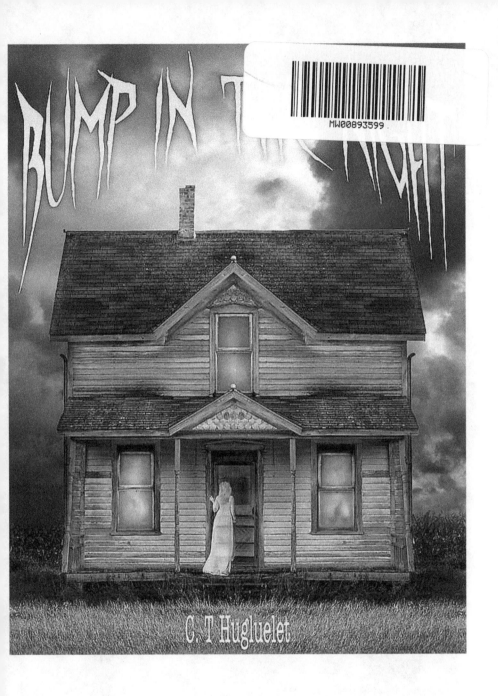

BUMP IN THE NIGHT

C. T Hugluelet

outskirts
press

Outskirts Press, Inc.
http://www.outskirtspress.com

ISBN: 978-1-9772-0286-4

Cover Image © 2021 Bigstock Photo

Outskirts Press and the "OP" logo are trademarks belonging to Outskirts Press, Inc.

PRINTED IN THE UNITED STATES OF AMERICA

This is for my two sons, Lance and Brian, and my two grandsons, Lance Joe and Leland Creed, but most of all, this is for Jerry, the love of my life that has been by my side for the past twenty nine years.

I don't believe that ghosts are "spirits of the dead" because I don't believe in death. In the multiverse, once you're possible, you exist. And once you exist, you exist forever one way or another. Besides, death is the absence of life, and the ghosts I've met are very much alive. What we call ghosts are life forms just as you and I are.

PAUL F. ENO, *Footsteps in the Attic*

———⟫⟪(◍)⟫⟪———

Prologue

Thinking back, Carl remembered how hard life was when he was younger. His father John Stanczyk, was an alcoholic. He regularly beat Carl, his brother Ray, and his mother. Caroline did something that women never did back in the thirties. She took her children and divorced John.

Carl left school in the eighth grade to help support his mother. At first he sold news paper and then helped deliver groceries. Even though he lacked schooling, Carl had an unbelievable set of mathematical skills. At sixteen he was hired as a machinist. He worked for the Litton Company on Western Ave. in Chicago until he was drafted. When WWII ended, Carl returned to the company that he had worked for as a machinist before the war. Caroline, his mother, had remarried and moved out of the city to the small suburban town of Westmont. Carl decided that now was a good time to look for a wife and settle down.

It would be nearly ten years after Carl returned home before he would meet who he would consider, the one.

Dorothy was three years younger than Carl. She was the third eldest of thirteen children. Also in her thirties, Dorothy had never been married.

They met at the Polonia Grove Ballroom off of Archer Ave. in Chicago. Dorothy loved to dance the polka, she had even won awards for her dancing. The two dated for a year and then married.

They were renting a flat on 25th and Avers, which was a few blocks from Dorothy's mother. The two had their first child Philip in 1956. Two years later Magdalene was born.

Carl was called into the foremen's office. The company recently opened a second plant in Downers Grove. They informed him that being one of their lead machinists he was going to be transferred to the new facility. He accepted, not really having a choice in the matter. Now Carl needed to break the news to Dorothy. Her parents had immigrated to Chicago from Poland. Dorothy had always lived in the city, her whole family did. Carl wasn't sure how she would take the news.

Before telling his wife, Carl decided to talk to his brother Ray, who also lived in Westmont. Ray was a volunteer firemen and a member on the Board of Trustees for the Village. Carl thought that he could recommend a place that they could call home.

"I do know of a place that the county is trying to sell. Their asking $15,000 for it. That is below the list price for this neighborhood," Ray told Carl.

"Why so low, Is there something wrong with it?" Carl questioned.

"No, I think the main reason is that the house does need some work. It's an older frame house that was built in the twenties," Ray said.

"Okay, what else? I don't think that your telling me everything," Carl told him.

"Well, I have heard that the man that owned the house died in some sort of accident on the job. A lot of people have said that he wasn't a very nice person. They've also said that his wife fell down the back steps on her way to the basement to do the laundry. Some people even think that it may not have been an accident. They think that he actually pushed her. When she fell, she broke her neck," Ray explained.

"I can't tell Dorothy that, she'll never set foot in that house," Carl said.

"You don't have to tell her that. The county sells houses all the time when there's no other family to claim the home," Ray told him.

"I've never lied to her," Carl informed him.

"You wouldn't be lying," Ray said. "You just wouldn't be telling her that part of it. Look... why don't you at least go see it. The house has a lot of potential. Your good with your hands. You can enclose the back stair so that she'd never have to walk outside to go down to the basement. There's also an old cistern under the stairs that hasn't been used in years, you can fill that in."

Ray was right the house did have a lot of potential regardless of what may have happened there. It was also three blocks away from his mother's house so she would be able to help Dorothy with the kids if needed. The train station was even closer. Dorothy had planned on going back to her old job once the kids were in school full time. Carl needed to make a decision soon. His company needed him in the other plant.

Carl made it home just in time for dinner. "I'm home," he announced as he gave Dorothy a kiss.

"How's Ray and your mother doing? Did you tell them that we want to have them over for dinner soon?" Dorothy said, when she noticed the look on Carl's face. "What is it Honey?"

"Sit down, I need to talk to you ," he told her. "I was called into the foremen's office the other day," Carl explained. "I'm being transferred to the Downers Grove plant."

"Where exactly is Downers Grove?" Dorothy asked.

"Actually it is right next to Westmont where my mother lives," he told her.

"I know that you don't have a choice, but isn't that going to be a long drive, day in and day out?" Dorothy asked.

Now came the part where he had to tell her about moving out of the city and away from her family.

Dorothy just sat in silence for awhile before she spoke up. "My place is with my husband. It doesn't matter what my family thinks about it. If it were them, they would do whatever they needed too, without considering my opinion."

Feeling relieved, Carl went on to tell her about the fruit trees in the back yard. "I know how much you love to bake. Oh....and the back yard is even big enough to invite your whole family when we have cook outs."

"Okay....okay, you've convinced me," Dorothy said as she laughed.

Carl was still worried, her younger sister Sophie had a mouth and she didn't mind voicing her opinion when necessary.

"When do we move?" Dorothy asked.

"There's some work that I want to do in the house before we actually move in. So when I get off of work I'll go straight there until I finish what needs to be done."

Carl had the lumber store deliver all the necessary materials to the new house. Every day after work he would go there and do as much work as he could. He usually stayed until sundown. One day in particular something strange happened. Carl couldn't shake the feeling that he was being watched. During the war he fought in the jungles of the Philippines where you were trained to be aware of your surroundings, but now he needed to remind himself that he wasn't in the jungle anymore, this was the suburbs. He continued to work, when he felt a breeze and then a hand on his shoulder. Startled, he turned quickly to see who was behind him and saw that no one was no there. Carl went back to framing out the window that he was putting in around the cistern when something caught his eye. In the dirt that cover the floor of the cistern he saw what appeared to be two cats eye marbles. Reaching in, he picked them up and thought, "these may be worth something. I think I'll save them for

Philip when he gets older." Brushing the dirt off, he slid them into his pocket.

He reached behind him to pick up the hammer, but it wasn't where he left it. Carl stood up to look for it when something grazed his left shoulder before crashing to the ground. Jumping back, he looked and saw that it was the hammer he had been looking for. Just a few inches more to the left and it would have split his skull wide open.

"Where the hell did that come from?" He said out loud. Looking all around to see if anyone else was there, Carl looked up at the top step thinking to himself, "could I have possibly left it up there?" Although he didn't recall going upstairs for any reason, nor would he have left it that far from his reach, but that was the only logical explanation he could come up with.

It took another three weeks to finish the enclosure. Carl decided to fill in the cistern another time. He just wanted to get his family moved into their new house.

Carl would often think about the incident with the hammer. He was a logical man, but he would have no idea how often his logic would be challenged in the time to come.

Part 1

A New Beginning, The Unexplained, and a Life Changed Forever

Chapter 1

D orothy was picking fruit in the back yard. She was going to make one of her famous apple pies. She had to admit, she didn't think that she would like living in the suburbs. Dorothy was a city girl born and raised. All of her family still lived there, but she loved living in Westmont, so did the kids. Her and Carl had planned on having a much bigger family, but after Magdalene was born over five years ago Dorothy just wasn't able to get pregnant. She had always planned on going back to her old job at Western Electric after the kids were in school full time. Magdalene was starting first grade next week so they decided that now would be a good time for her to go back to work. Carl was going on second shift so Dorothy could work first.

Just then Magdalene came racing through the yard, "Mommy, Mommy, Mom, Mom."

"What is it Sweetie?"

"I was at Miss Gerlando's house. She has two cats, BoBo kitty and Smokey. Can we have a cat Mom? Please!"

"Magdalene we already have a dog."

"But a dog isn't a cat. I want a cat mom," Magdalene insisted.

"I'll talk to your father about it," Dorothy already knew what Carl would say.

"Yah, we're getting a cat," Magdalene shouted. Running back to

Miss Gerlando's house. Alls Dorothy could do was smile and shake her head.

"Did I just hear Magdalene cheering because we're getting a cat?" Carl asked, walking out the back door with his lunch box in his hand.

"She's over at Gracie's playing with her cats, and now Magdalene has decided that she wants one," Dorothy explained. "I already knew want the answer would be, but I told her that I would talk to you about it."

"Sorry Honey, but the answer is no. We already have a dog."

"Give it a couple of weeks and she'll forget all about it, then she'll be onto something else," Dorothy told him.

"Alright.....I'm leaving for work. If you have any problems I'm only ten minutes away," Carl reminded her.

"Every time you say that it scares me. It makes me feel like something bad is going to happen," Dorothy told him.

"I'm sorry," Carl told her as he kissed her on the cheek. After he got in the car he watched her for a minute as she picked apples off the tree. He knew how easily some things frightened her. Carl just never forgot, when he first started working on the house his hammer seemed to have just fallen out of the sky missing his head by inches. Normally he didn't let things like that bother him. He had survived the war, hell he had even survived the days of Al Capone and prohibition. Remembering back to when he was seven years old, Carl had saved his pennies to buy some candy. On the way to the store a car rounded the corner at high speed. A man with a Tommy gun opened fire on the store he was about to go into. Running as fast as he could Carl took cover behind a bush. So why the hell did that damn hammer bother him so much? If the truth be told, just being on that side of the house gave him the heebie jeebies.

Dorothy fed the kids, gave them their bathes, and got them ready for bed. After the kids fell asleep was when her and Carl would spend their time together. Now that he was on second shift, Dorothy felt a little lost. At nine o'clock she decided to go to bed.

Magdalene awoke when she heard a voice, actually she heard a lot voices. It was hard to tell what they were saying, the voices were all jumbled. Starting to feel frightened, she pulled the covers up over her head and prayed. Magdalene's mother always told her, "whenever you feel scared, just say a little prayer and God will protect you."

She lay there and waited for the voices to stop. Just as Magdalene was about to fall asleep she heard what sounded like someone playing with her new game Ker plunk. She could hear the sound of marbles falling. Getting up, she tip toed to the bedroom door to look out and see if it might be Philip playing with her game. When Magdalene looked, no one was out there. Running back to her bed, she dove under the covers and hid. She finally fell asleep, she was just too exhausted to keep her eyes open any longer.

When Magdalene awoke her parents were sitting at the kitchen table drinking their coffee.

"Well....there she is," Carl announced.

"You must have slept good last night, it's after eight," Dorothy added.

"Mom, Dad, I heard people talking in my room last night," Magdalene told them.

"What people Sweetie?" Dorothy asked.

"I don't know. There was a lot of them, but I couldn't understand what they were saying. Their voices were all jumbled," Magdalene said.

"Magdalene, there was probably a soft ball game going on at the park last night. Those were the voices you heard," Carl explained. Even though he didn't quite believe it himself as he was saying it. The field was about five blocks away. You wouldn't be able to hears any voices from that distance, and on a Monday night. They didn't have Monday night games.

"Well....what about my game Ker plunk. I heard someone playing with it last night. I thought that it was Philip, but when I looked no one was there," Magdalene said.

"It was probably just the mice in the wall," Carl told her. "They can make noise sometimes."

Magdalene's eyes got as big as saucers. "There are mice that live in our walls?"

"Honey, it's probably just one. Every house has them," Carl told her.

"Well....do they wear heavy boots? Cause they sure are noisy," Magdalene informed them. "If we had a cat, we wouldn't have any mice. He can sleep in my room too, then I wouldn't be scared."

"I guess I walked right into that one," Carl said, as he laughed.

"Sweetie every house creaks and groans, it's just the noise a house makes when it settles. You're always going to hear some sort of bump in the night," Dorothy told her. "There's nothing to be afraid of."

Magdalene, although reluctant, seemed to except her parents explanation. Dorothy thought that would be the end of it. Magdalene would be in school next week. Dorothy was sure that she would be too busy with school work and making new friends to worry about hearing any noises. Unfortunately the voices didn't stop for Magdalene.

The first week of school went well for both of the kids. Dorothy was a little concerned since she was returning back to work next week. Dorothy knew that she would do nothing but worry about them at work, and if that was the case it would have been better for her to just stay home, but with the cost of food and clothing going up constantly, the extra money would help.

It was sometime in October when Magdalene started to hear the noises again. She had been too tired since school started to notice them. Now there appeared to be other noises that she'd never heard before. Magdalene thought that she heard someone changing the channel to the television set in the front room. It went click, click, click, the same noise the dial made when it was being turned. Tip toeing to her bedroom door, she looked out, but there was no one there. The television wasn't even on. Running back to her bed, she hid under the covers and said a prayer.

After awhile the noise stopped. Pulling the covers back, Magdalene lay there trying to fall back asleep, when she looked toward the closet and saw the doorknob turning back and forth making a clicking noise. This time she jumped out of bed and ran down the hall to her parents room where her mother was asleep. Magdalene was afraid to go in, she didn't want her mother to get angry. She stood outside the room for what seemed like forever when she finally tip toed in, and slid into the bed without waking her mother.

When Magdalene awoke she was in her own bed. Sitting there, she looked around and wondered if it had all been a dream. She walked into the kitchen and sat down at the table to have breakfast. Her mother had already left for work.

"Morning Sweetheart."

"Morning Daddy."

"Did you have a bad dream last night? I saw that you were in our bed last night," Carl asked.

"I heard noises last night," Magdalene replied.

"I thought that I explained to you what was causing them," Carl said.

"These were different," Magdalene told her father. "It sounded like someone was changing the channels on the television."

"Honey, it was probably the furnace turning on and off," Carl said.

"Then tell me why the doorknob on my closet was turning back and forth?" Magdalene asked, as she made a turning motion with her hand.

Carl sighed, he was running out of explanations to tell her. "It was probably your eyes playing tricks on you. Now finish your breakfast. You and your brother have to get ready for school."

Magdalene stomped down the hall in a huff, "nobody believes me."

More and more Carl would come home to find Magdalene in their bed. Sometimes he would carry her back to her own bed and other times he was tired and it was just easier for him to sleep in her room.

Philip and Magdalene were excited, Christmas was finally here. Getting ready to go to their Grandmother's house, they set out a plate of cookies and a glass of milk before they left.

Magdalene loved the time that she spent with her Grandma, but she couldn't wait to get home. Her Grandma always gave her the same thing for Christmas, bloomers and socks. She knew that the good stuff was at home. When they got there, Santa did not disappoint. Magdalene got a Easy Bake Oven and a Barbie Doll. Philip got some Match Box Cars and a model airplane.

There was one special gift under the tree for Magdalene. Dorothy found a ceramic cat figurine at the Drug Store's gift shop. She knew how much Magdalene wanted a cat, so she felt that this would be the next best thing.

When Magdalene opened the gift from her mother, she jumped up and down, "thank-you Mommy, thank-you so much. I love it," she squealed.

"I thought that you could set him next to your bed so he can keep you company at night," Dorothy told her. Hoping that would keep her in her own bed at night.

"That's a great idea Mommy. That's exactly what I'll do," Magdalene boasted. "I think I'll call him Mittens."

Mittens was a success. The thought of him being there at night kept Magdalene sleeping in her own bed for the next three months, until Carl and Dorothy were awaken by a scream.

Running down the hall into Magdalene's room, they saw her huddled in the corner of her bed with the covers pulled up around her neck.

"What's the matter Sweetie? Did you have a bad dream?" Carl asked.

"Mittens is gone." Magdalene cried, pointing to the empty night stand. "I was sleeping and I felt someone touching my hair and when I looked to see who it was, Mittens was gone," she whimpered.

"You can sleep with Mommy tonight and I'll sleep in your bed. We'll look for Mittens in the morning," Carl told her. "I promise."

He looked at Dorothy and told her, "remind me to check the furnace in the morning. It's freezing in this room."

Magdalene was still asleep when Dorothy got up. She walked down the hall to Magdalene's room to find Carl on his hands and knees looking under the bed for Mittens. "I can't find him anywhere. It's a damn ceramic cat, it didn't just grow legs and walk out of here," Carl snapped.

"What are we going to tell her? She loved that cat," Dorothy asked.

"I don't like to lie, but if we tell her that we can't find him, she'll never set foot in this room again. So....I'll tell her that when he fell on the floor he broke into a lot of little pieces that I can't put back together."

That was the end of Mittens, no one ever found him.

Chapter 2

It took a while for Magdalene to get over the loss of Mittens, but she tried to be brave. It wasn't often, but every now and again Carl would come home to find her in their bed. He really didn't get angry, he knew that she was trying.

They decided to get the kids involved in music. When Carl was a young adult he played the saxophone and clarinet, while his brother Ray played the concertina. Magdalene wanted to play the flute, but as she put it, "I can't get this thing to work." Instead she would play the clarinet and Philip would play the trumpet. While the kids were occupied with their instruments, Dorothy took that opportunity to do things around the house. She liked keeping busy. Dorothy would leave work, take the train, and when it pulled into the station she would walk the two blocks home. After making dinner she would get the kids ready for bed after they did their home work.

Even though things were going great, Dorothy noticed the she was becoming easily irritated and frequently exhausted. She didn't dare tell Carl, because she knew what he'd say. His words rang out like a bell, "you know, you don't have to work." The truth was, Dorothy liked the thought of being able to contribute to the household. It gave her the feeling of independents.

It was a typical Saturday morning. The kids hurried through their breakfast. Racing into the front room to watch television, they argued over who was better, Daffy Duck or Bugs Bunny. Carl ignored the world while he read his news paper.

Dorothy went downstairs to do the laundry. Sitting down, she began to sort through the clothes for the tenth time. Magdalene had deemed herself the official product tester. The Tide laundry commercial showed a women washing her clothes, and when she finished, she found a sock that was left inside of another sock, but miraculously it was clean. "Thanks to the power of Tide." Trying to find out if it was true Magdalene would shove socks inside of pants pockets and other socks, saying, "Mom don't worry, they'll be clean. That's what the lady in the commercial says."

While sitting there Dorothy heard a faint voice, a little girl saying, "Mommy are you there? Can you hear me?" She called out, "Magdalene, is that you?" Dorothy waited a second, when there was no response she brushed it off as being her imagination. Putting the laundry in the machine Dorothy heard, "Mommy, I'm so cold. Help me, I can't get out." Dorothy shouted, "I'm coming Magdalene, where are you?"

Carl heard Dorothy shout. Putting down his paper, he went down stairs to see what was wrong, "what is it Honey? I heard you shouting all the way upstairs."

"It was Magdalene, she needed my help," Dorothy replied.

Magdalene's upstairs, she's watching TV," Carl told her.

"I thought I heard her calling for help," Dorothy said.

Carl gave Dorothy a strange look, "are you sure that your okay?"

She started to sway back and forth. Carl grabbed her and sat her in the chair. "I've just been feeling a little tired lately," she told him.

"I told you that you didn't have to go back to work," the both of them saying it at the same time.

"I'm fine," Dorothy told him. "I just get a little tired every now and then, but I do want to make an appointment with Dr. Hall. It wouldn't hurt to have a check up."

"Good....see if you can get in to see him Monday, I'll take you," Carl replied.

Dr. Hall had a cancellation for 10am, so Dorothy took it. While sitting there Dorothy felt a pang of uneasiness, "what if something is wrong?" she thought.

Dr. Hall was his usual jovial self. He had been Carl and Dorothy's doctor since they moved to Westmont. "So what brings you here today? I haven't seen you in awhile."

Dorothy explained that she was feeling exhausted and irritable, she even included hearing the voice calling out to her. Dorothy had debated whether or not to tell him about the voices Magdalene had heard, but she decided against it.

Dr. Hall explained to her that when people get exhausted, sometimes the mind can play tricks on a person. He motioned for her to sit on the examining table, "I want to give you a complete check up since you haven't been here in awhile." When he finished his exam, he told her, "you can get dressed and go out into the waiting room. I'd like to talk to Carl."

The doctor told Carl to sit down. After a long pause he finally spoke, "I found a lump in Dorothy's left breast."

"A lump," Carl said. "What kind of lump"

"I won't know until after the surgery, but it could be cancer."

"Cancer." Carl felt like someone had just punched him in the gut knocking the wind out of him.

Dr. Hall held up his hand, "I'm not saying that it is, but if it is we need to take care of it now. There have been a lot of advancements in the treatment of cancer. If we have to remove her breast, we would give her a series of cobalt treatments, which is radiation. Depending on how advanced the cancer is, we may also remove her ovaries. If we can eliminate the estrogen that her body produces it could stop the cancer from spreading."

Sitting there stunned, Carl finally spoke up. "I thought you said that you weren't sure that it was cancer. Now you're talking like it is."

"It may not be, but judging by the other symptoms I think that it is," Dr. Hall told him.

"What am I going to tell her?" Carl asked.

"Tell her as little as possible, I'll handle the rest," he told Carl.

Carl went out into the waiting room fearing that Dorothy would read the expression on his face. "What did the doctor say to you?" Dorothy asked.

"Come on....I'll tell you in the car," Carl had no idea what he was going to say. When they got in the car he looked at her and said, "the doctor found a lump in your breast."

"A lump." Dorothy's voice started to break up, then tears began to well up in her eyes.

"They want to operate and take it out, they need to make sure that it isn't cancer." Carl left it at that, and held her as she cried.

Things were moving fast. Dr. Hall wanted Dorothy in the hospital within a week. Carl made the necessary arrangements. His foremen told him to take as much time as he needed. Carl had been with the company for over twenty years so it wasn't a problem. His mother told him that she would take care of the kids while Dorothy was in the hospital.

On the day of the surgery, as they were wheeling her to the operating room Carl kissed her and said, "everything is going to be okay. I'll see you when you get back to your room." There was something that bothered him. He had a gut feeling that things wouldn't be okay.

It was now going on five hours since Dorothy was taken into surgery. Carl was losing his mind not knowing what they were doing to her. Just as he was going to find a nurse, Dr. Hall came through the doors.

"How's Dorothy, Is my wife okay?"

"Carl sit down," Dr Hall said.

"Is my wife okay," Carl persisted.

"She's in recovery. I'm sorry Carl, it was a lot worst then I thought. We took her left breast and the lymph nodes under her arm an additional tissue. While she was under, we decided to take her ovaries."

Carl didn't know how to respond. With tears in his eyes he finally said, "is she going to die?"

All that Dr. Hall would say was, "I think we got it all."

"What am I going to tell her?" He asked.

"I'll be there with you when she wakes up. I'll explain it to her."

After the doctor left the room Carl held Dorothy as she cried. There was nothing he or anyone could say that could change any of this. He just knew that he loved her and whispered in her ear, "we'll get through this together."

Dorothy spent the next three weeks in the hospital, she was determined to fight and willing to do whatever it took to get through it. She had a few more cobalt treatments to go through before they would let her go home.

Carl was finishing up on the repairs to the lawn mower. He told Magdalene, "go in the house and get my watch off the dresser. I need to watch the time."

"Is it going somewhere?" Magdalene asked curiously.

"No Honey, I mean that I need to know how late it's getting so that I can see your mother when visiting hour start."

"Oh....okay," she said. Skipping up the sidewalk to the back door. Magdalene grabbed the watch off her father's dresser. Sliding it on her wrist, she liked pretending she was a grown up. Magdalene would always go into her mother's closet and try on all of her high heel shoes, then parade around the house until her mother yelled at her, "put my shoes back in the closet where you found them."

Walking down the back steps she felt a strange chill, there were two more steps to go when Magdalene felt someone push her. Instinctively she put her arms out to break the fall when her left arm went through the glass of the storm door. In a panic she pulled her arm out and stood outside afraid to move. She just knew that her father was going to be mad at her for breaking the glass in the door.

Carl was growing impatient, "I should have gotten the watch myself," he muttered out loud. He walked out the garage door and started up the sidewalk when he saw Magdalene standing there holding her arm that was now covered in blood. He ran over to her and saw the broken glass, "Sweetie what happened?" Gently taking her arm to see how bad it was.

"Someone pushed me," she said. Her bottom lip started to quiver.

Carl got angry, firmly grabbing her shoulders he said, "no one pushed you, there was no one in the house. I don't need this shit right now not with your mother in the hospital."

Just then Mrs. Shoemocker the next door neighbor ran over with a towel in her hand, "is she okay? I saw what happened."

"I need to get her up to Dr. Kernicki's office. He's in town, it'll be closer. Can you keep an eye on Philip for me?"

"Yes....just go. Philip will be fine," she said.

Carl grabbed Magdalene, he carried her in his arms as he cut through some of the neighbors yards on the way to town. It was faster that way.

Dr. Kernicki had just finished with the last of his patients when Carl came through the door. Without hesitation he took them into his office. He didn't like to stitch up children. They tended to scream and fight which made it harder. He knew Magdalene was scared, but he also saw an incredible inner strength for such a young child to have. It took eight stitches to close the wound on her arm. The doctor told Carl to bring her back in two weeks so he could take them out. He also informed Carl that she would probably have a nasty scar, but it should fade over time.

They left the doctor's office and walked over to the dime store. Carl felt bad that he scolded Magdalene. He knew that she truly believed that she was pushed, but with Dorothy being sick he just couldn't deal with anything else. Carl told her that she could pick out anything that she wanted for being so brave.

Magdalene walked up to the counter where her father was waiting for her and put a little flower pot on the counter that held seven tiny pink plastic roses.

"Are you sure that's what you want?" Carl asked. It seemed like such a strange thing for her to pick out.

"Yes Daddy, I want you to give them to Mommy when you visit her today," she said smiling.

"That is a great idea. She'll love it," Carl said giving her a hug.

Carl presented Dorothy with the flower pot that Magdalene picked out for her. It brought tears to her eyes. Instead of her little girl getting something for herself, she thought of giving her mother a gift.

There was even better news. The doctors told Dorothy that she was responding very well to the treatment and would be able to go home in a couple of days. Dorothy also told Carl that the doctor said it would be okay for her to return to work in a few months.

"Sweetheart, I told you that you don't need to work," Carl reminded her.

"I know, but I want too. All these medical bills are going to cost more than we have," Dorothy told him.

Carl felt himself getting angry. He wanted his wife home. He wanted her to get well. He knew money would be tight, but Dorothy's health was more important. Carl was about to tell her that his mind was made up when Dr. Hall came through the door.

"So did Dorothy tell you the good news?" Dr. Hall boasted. "She'll be leaving us in a couple of days."

"Yes she told me," Carl said gritting his teeth.

The nurse came in and asked the both of them to step out of the room so that she could change Dorothy's bandage.

This was Carl's chance. He asked Dr. Hall, "what were you thinking? You told Dorothy that she could go back to work!"

"Listen Carl, I know that I should have spoke with you first, but I think that it important for Dorothy to live her life out how ever she wants to."

"What do you mean, live her life out? I thought that you told her that the treatments were working? What are you not telling me?" Carl shot back.

"She is responding. We don't always know if cancer will return once we remove it, but it is important for a person to remain active. It helps in the healing process. If it becomes necessary, we can always do additional cobalt treatments periodically, just as a precaution."

Carl felt like he was fighting a losing battle, Dorothy wanted to work and Dr. Hall was no help. He had no choice but to go along with what the doctor was saying.

Walking through the front door, Dorothy was the happiest she'd been in awhile. She was home. Dorothy had been afraid that she would never see her home or her children again.

Magdalene was nervous. She didn't know what it meant to be operated on. Was her mother going to be different? Would she look different? There were so many questions that she didn't know the answer to, but the minute she saw her mother walk through the door Magdalene ran and give her mother a big hug, "Mommy I missed you so much. I'm glad your home."

"Me too Sweetie, me too," Dorothy whispered.

Dorothy didn't let the surgery she had slow her down. She picked fruit from the trees in the back yard and baked pies.

"You need to slow down a little," Carl warned. I don't want you to hurt yourself trying to do too much."

"I'll be fine," Dorothy assured him.

While Dorothy was getting dressed in the morning, Magdalene came down the hallway. She saw that her mother's bedroom door was open. Facing the mirror as she tried to put her bra on, Dorothy was totally unaware that Magdalene was watching. She stood there horrified when she saw what they had done to her mother. The left side of her mother's chest was completely gone, it even looked as if it was caved in. There was a continuous thick red scar that went from the front of her, under her mother's left arm and up her shoulder blade in the back. Magdalene backed up and tip toed back down the hall so her mother wouldn't see her. Sitting on the edge of the bed, she stared blankly at the wall. She realized that her mother was different. Someone had butchered her. Afraid that her mother would see that she was upset, Magdalene yelled down the hall, "Mommy, can I go outside and play?"

"Did you make your bed?" Dorothy replied.

"Yes."

"Stay close to the house then."

Magdalene ran out of the house and under the front porch steps and cried. She didn't want her mother to see her. Magdalene was afraid that it would make her feel bad if she know the reason why. Ten minutes had gone by when she finally stopped crying. She decided that, since her mother was so brave, she needed to be brave too.

Dorothy's body was physically healing, but emotionally her mind was racing. She kept playing over and over in her mind what Dr. Hall had told her, "your responding well to the treatment....we got all of the tumor," but it just didn't' set right. This was cancer, people died from cancer all the time. What if she was dying? They had two small children. The county wasn't going to let a single man raise two children on his own. Dorothy knew that his mother and hers for that matter were up in age, and most of her brothers and sisters already had four and five children each. She just knew that Philip and Magdalene would wind up in a home. Dorothy was terrified, she had no idea what those places were like.

Frantic, Dorothy ran out to the garage. "I need to talk to you Carl."

"What's wrong....are you feeling okay?" Rushing to Dorothy's side.

"Carl what if the doctors are wrong? What if I die? What will happen to the kids?"

"Honey, you're not going to die." Carl tried to assure her.

"It happens, people die from cancer all the time. What if the county takes the kids?"

"They're not going to. I won't let them."

"You may not have a say in it, you'll be a single man trying to raise two small children." Dorothy insisted.

"Stop!" Carl finally said. I promise you, I'll take care of our children." He knew that there was no point in arguing.

"I need to know what those places are like," Dorothy told him, almost begging.

"You want to visit an orphanage?" Carl was stunned at her request.

"Yes, I need to see for myself what their like," Dorothy replied.

Carl went to see his brother Ray. He didn't even know where to begin, so he came right out and told Ray about Dorothy's request. They both understood that her life had changed, there were things that would never be that same. Carl knew that there was the possibility that she could die. Since Ray worked for the village he did know of an orphanage about forty five minutes outside of town. He told Carl that he would call Monday morning and find out if they would allow them to visit.

Ray called Carl Monday afternoon and let him know that they could visit the home next Saturday.

"I want the kids to come with us," Dorothy told him.

"What are we going to tell them? What possible reason do we have to visit an orphanage?" Carl protested.

"We'll tell them that we're visiting kids that are less fortunate then they are, because they don't have any family. I know you don't understand, I just need to see what those places are like. What if something happens to me or the both of us, and neither one of our families can take Philip and Magdalene. Wouldn't you want to know that they're not in a bad place?"

Carl nodded, there was nothing else that he could say.

On the way there, Dorothy told the kids where they were going and her explanation to why. Philip and Magdalene seemed to except what she told them and didn't ask any questions.

Pulling into the parking lot, they drove up to a huge three story building surrounded by trees that sat on perfectly manicured grounds, that spanned over five acres of land. They were allowed to walk around freely. The different floors were divided up into dormitories, by age groups and genders. It didn't appear to be over crowded, actually there didn't seem to be a lot of children there, but they all looked like they had been well cared for. The building was clean and maintained. Dorothy had expected to see a lot more children, but when she didn't, she hoped it was because that meant there were families that were willing to care for and love the children that had no one. Dorothy never wanted her children to ever have to go into an orphanage, but at least she was satisfied that it wasn't like the story of Oliver Twist and the other orphans that had to beg for a second helping of food.

Chapter 3

At some point Dorothy actually started to believe that she was going to survive her illness. She was feeling better every day, her body was healing and she was returning to work next month. All the medical bills were taking a toll on their finances, but Carl never complained once. He was just happy that Dorothy was getting better. Dorothy regretted putting Carl through such an emotional roller coaster ride. A lot of men wouldn't have stood for it, but Carl never left her side. Dorothy just knew that she had plenty of time to make it up to him.

Sitting in the kitchen, Dorothy was talking on the phone to her sister Helene. Magdalene stomped down the hall, stopped and put her hands on her hips, "Mom the news man interrupted the Flintstones. I can't watch my cartoons because he said something bad happened."

"Oh my God, not again," Dorothy said under her breath.

"What is it?" Helene asked.

"I'm not sure, the last time they interrupted Magdalene's cartoons with a news bulletin was when JFK was shot. I have to go, just turn on your TV set," Dorothy told Helene.

Dorothy sat down on the couch and listened while the reporter told the world that an unidentified male had just slain eight student nurses in their townhome near Chicago. While listening in horror,

Carl walked through the door with Philip. They had been playing catch out back. "Carl you need to hear this," Dorothy yelled down the hall.

"What is it?" Sitting next to Dorothy, Carl listened to the details.

The police showed a sketch of the male suspect, stating that, "this individual also has a tattoo on his forearm that reads Born To Raise Hell." They went on to say, "the suspect broke into the home belonging to nine student nurses. While taking his victims into different rooms it is believed that he lost count of how many women were actually there, allowing one of the women to hide under the bed undetected. She then climbed out of the second story window once she was sure he had gone, then proceeded to scream for help. This is the most brutal crime that Chicago has seen in decades. If anyone knows the whereabouts of this individual, contact the Chicago police department immediately. Do not try and apprehend this person. He is believed to be armed and dangerous."

Dorothy grabbed Carl's arm, "You don't think he'll wind up in our town, do you?"

"No I don't think so. We're over forty miles away. He's probably hiding somewhere in Chicago." Carl assured her.

"Mom, Dad, is that bad man going to come here?" Philip and Magdalene asked almost simultaneously.

"No, there is no bad man coming here. Do you two understand me?" Carl firmly stated.

"Yes Daddy," they both replied.

"I'm so glad we moved away from the city." Dorothy added.

The whole city of Chicago was on edge including the surrounding areas. No one was going to rest easy until the killer was caught. Two days after his murder spree, it was announced that, "twenty four year old Richard Benjamin Speck was arrested for the murders of the eight student nurses. He was apprehended at Cook County Hospital after a failed suicide attempt."

Dorothy breathed a sigh of relief, the same as everyone else. Luckily enough the kids had already put it out of their minds.

Dorothy was getting herself ready to go back to work. They didn't have much extra in the way of money, but she needed to at least get a couple of new dresses. Since the surgery she had to dress a little differently now. Dorothy knew how to sew, which was helpful. She planned on altering some of her other dresses after the kids went to bed. Magdalene was brushing her teeth when Dorothy called out, "did you put your bike away like I told you too?"

"No Mommy, I forgot."

"When you finish brushing your teeth I want you to put your bike under the front porch. I mean it, or you're going to be in trouble with your father if someone takes it."

Magdalene peeked out the front door. It was dark out, but not scary dark. Walking up to her bike that was laying on the front lawn, she glanced over to the lilac bushes. They lined the opposite side of the walkway that ran the length of the house. The lilac bushes were more like trees, they had grown over twelve feet tall and arched over the walkway towards the right side of the house. Something caught Magdalene's attention. It appeared to be a small shadowy figure. At first she thought it might be Philip planning to scare her. Slowly creeping up to the bushes, Magdalene smiled as she called out to her brother, "Philip I know it's you." When she approached the bushes, now facing the figure, she realized that it didn't look like her brother. It didn't even look real. All of a sudden a dark boney hand reached out to grab her. Screaming, Magdalene ran towards the front door. Dorothy could hear her scream all the way into the kitchen.

Magdalene burst through the door screaming, "Mommy someone tried to grab me behind the bushes out there."

"Did you see who it was?"

"No, I thought it was Philip."

Without thinking, Dorothy ran out the front door around to the side of the house where Magdalene said that she saw someone. She looked behind the bushes and in the back yard, but she didn't see anything out of place.

When Dorothy came back in she found Magdalene huddled with her brother in his bedroom. "Did you see him Mommy?" Magdalene jumped off of the bed running towards Dorothy.

"No Sweetie, I didn't see anyone."

"But he was out there, behind the bushes. I saw him, I thought it was Philip."

"It wasn't me," Philip cut in.

"I know it wasn't. Magdalene I need you to tell me exactly what you saw."

"The closer I got to the shadow the funnier it started to look."

"Was he short or tall?" Dorothy probed.

"Like the size of Philip, when I got closer whoever it was looked like they were covered in dirt, kinda fuzzy, like there was a shadow around them. When they reached out to me, the hand looked dark and boney."

"I'm calling your father."

Dorothy phoned Carl and explained what happened. Slamming the receiver down, Carl got in his car and drove home. Before going in Carl looked around the yard first, then he put Magdalene's bike under the steps. When he walked in the house he went over to Magdalene and asked her the same questions that Dorothy did. Magdalene repeated the same words almost exactly the same way she had when her mother questioned her, never changing her story.

Dorothy pulled Carl aside and asked, "you don't think it had anything to do with the nurses that were killed?"

"They caught the guy that did it, Honey," Carl reminded her.

"What if there was more than one guy involved?"

"There wasn't, remember there was a witness," Carl told her. "I'm going back outside to look around some more with a flashlight."

"Just be careful," Dorothy warned.

Carl went back outside and walked back and forth shinning the flashlight on the ground behind the bushes, looking for anything that might indicate that someone was standing there, a cigarette butt, or a gum wrapper, something. Stopping suddenly, he noticed two small foot prints. It appeared that the person was barefoot. They were slightly bigger then Magdalene's feet and according to her, she never went behind the bushes. They were also facing in the wrong direction. It did seem like someone could have been watching her. Just then he heard a voice behind him. "Is everything alright?"

Jumping, Carl turned around with his flashlight raised in the air. Standing behind him was their other next store neighbor Ben Masters. "Whoa....whoa," Ben said raising his hands. "Sorry, I didn't mean to scare ya."

"Damn, actually you scared the shit out of me."

"I saw a light out here and I thought I heard your little girl scream earlier. Is everything okay?"

"I'm not sure. My wife told Magdalene to put her bike away, and when she came out here, she said that there was someone standing behind the bushes. I came back here to see if I could find any evidence that someone may have been hiding back here. You didn't by chance see or hear anything, did you?"

"No I didn't. I would have come out here right away if I did," Ben replied.

"Let me ask you something. Have you ever noticed anything strange out here? Did you know the people that lived here before us?"

"When we moved in, it was right after the man that owned your house died in an accident. Some of the people in town told me that he was a real SOB."

"I heard that too," Carl said, nodding his head.

"I also heard that he may have killed his wife. I did kinda see something odd one night," Ben said. "I heard some banging out here, and when I looked out the window there was some kinda fog over that cistern you put a wall around. To be real honest with ya, I kinnda get a chill that runs through me when I'm on this side of the house. It's almost like I get the feeling that someone's watching me."

Carl knew exactly what he meant, but decided not to tell him about the experience he had with the hammer.

Just then they heard the front door open, "is everything okay out there Carl?" Dorothy asked. She started to get worried because he had been gone so long.

"Everything's fine, I'm talking with Ben," Carl replied.

"Good evening Ben."

"Evening Dorothy."

When she went back into the house Carl let Ben know, "she doesn't know anything about what happened in that house before I bought it, and I want it to stay that way."

Ben assured Carl that he wouldn't say a word to her about it. "By the way, how is Dorothy doing? We heard that she was sick," Ben asked.

"She actually seems to be getting better," Carl said. Still trying to convince himself.

"Well you tell her that if she needs anything, don't hesitate to ask. Tell her to come on over and Ellen and I will be more than glad to do what we can."

"Thank-you Ben," Carl said shaking his hand.

Waking back into the house, Carl told Dorothy that he couldn't seem to find anything out of place. He also let her know that Ben and Ellen were more than happy to help out if she ever needed anything while he was at work. Carl suggested that she let Magdalene sleep with her and he would sleep in her bed when he got home. Carl had decide to go back to work and try and salvage the night.

Dorothy was starting to sense something, but couldn't quite put her finger on it.

Chapter 4

After returning back to work, Dorothy couldn't help but think about the night Magdalene saw someone behind the bushes. Although things like that did happen in their town, she still felt that Carl was keeping something from her. Dorothy knew that if she pressed him, he would tell her that she worried too much when there was nothing to be worried about. He was right, she did worry about everything, and did scare easily. Whenever there was a storm she would always take the kids downstairs until it was over. Carl would get so angry, he would say, "your scaring the kids, it's just a little thunder."

When Dorothy was younger, she had gone to visit her older sister Mary who lived in a garden apartment in the city. The weather got bad, but since it was so hot out Mary had the windows open. Suddenly a bolt of lightning shot through one of the open windows, bounced off of the floor and out the opposite open window. After that Dorothy was terrified of storms. She never drove either. Dorothy suffered from night blindness, her eyes played tricks on her in the dark. She always prayed the rosary when her and Carl drove anywhere. Dorothy had to admit to herself that she was frightened by the things that she didn't understand.

As a mother she earned the right to worry about her children. Philip was struggling with his school work. Dorothy wasn't sure if it was because she hadn't been able to devote as much time to helping him like she had before she became ill. Now that she was back at work, he really seemed to be having a hard time. It upset her when they attended family gatherings and some of her sisters didn't stop their kids from teasing Philip. He would cry, and as she tried to comfort him, it made her cry.

On Saturday Dorothy's brother Julius would take the train in from the city. Julius taught high school English. He told Dorothy that he would tutor Philip every Saturday until his grades went up. Magdalene would sit in, she pretended to be the teacher's assistant.

One thing Dorothy could always count on was seeing Magdalene's smiling face. She would ride her bike up to the corner and wait for Dorothy when she walked home from work. Sometimes Magdalene felt uneasy while she waited. Their neighbor Mr. Remic who lived on the opposite side of the street would leer at her.

Mr. and Mrs. Remic were and older couple that lived in the corner house. They kept to themselves and didn't appear to be very friendly. Mr. Remic was a retired gardener. No one really knew how old he was, his skin was so weathered by the sun it was impossible to tell. He was a smaller man that spent most of his time on his hands and knees tending to his lawn, pulling any weeds he could find.

Dorothy taught the kids never to be disrespectful to anyone. Although, Dorothy had to admit that she didn't quite care for him herself. Especially after he had scared Magdalene away when she was selling Girl Scout cookies.

Finishing her homework, Magdalene put her pencil down and asked, "Mom, would it be okay if I ride my bike before supper?"

"You can ride it for a little while, supper will be ready in a half an hour. Just don't get dirty, that's a new dress."

"Thank-you Mommy."

Racing out the front door, Magdalene heard, "walk don't run."

"Sorry Mommy."

Magdalene rode off on her bike. She never went far. Always riding around the same two blocks. This time she decided to go across the street. Magdalene didn't see Mr. Remic, she thought that he must have gone in the house. She didn't notice the rock laying next to the sidewalk in front of the Remic's house. When she rode around for the third time was when the front wheel of her bike hit the rock. The bike went out from under her, sending her crashing to the ground.

Trying not to scream out in pain, Magdalene grabbed her knee and rocked back and forth. Looking up, she saw Mr. Remic standing over her staring, "you need to be more careful," he growled. "You could have torn up my lawn falling like that. Look at ya, your knees bleeding." All's Magdalene could do was shake. Watching him bend over to look at her knee, she realized he seemed to be looking past it. When she followed his eyes to see what he was looking at was when she noticed that she had torn her dress and you could see her panties. Mr. Remic couldn't take his eyes off of them. Scooting back, Magdalene felt him grab her leg. Just then Mrs. Remic came out of the house, "what happened?"

"That little brat fall off her bike and almost tore up my grass," her husband said walking away.

"Come on child," Mrs. Remic said, helping Magdalene over to the steps. She noticed the rock and thought it was strange, because it belonged in the back yard by the garden. "You sit right here, I get you cleaned up and put a bandage on your knee." When Mrs. Remic came back, she had a cookie in one hand and a bandage in the other. Cleaning up Magdalene's knee, she let her finish the cookie before telling her to go home.

As she walked home, Magdalene was more afraid of what her mother was going to do to her for ripping her new dress. She remembered when her mother spanked her for cutting off her pedal pushers to make them into shorts, saying, "clothes are expensive, money doesn't grow on trees." Her and Philip rarely got spanked, but their mother always kept a belt on the table just to remind them what could happen if they misbehaved. Magdalene snapped out of her trance when she heard her mother's voice, "what happened to you? Just look at your dress."

"I'm sorry Mommy, I fell off my bike," Magdalene told her. Pointing to the Remic's house. "Mrs. Remic cleaned up my knee and put a bandage on it."

"She did?" Dorothy replied. She couldn't help but to sound surprised. Dorothy wondered, "could I have misjudged the Remics'."

"Mommy am I in trouble for ripping my dress?" Magdalene asked, almost afraid to find out the answer to that question.

"No Sweetie, it was an accident. I think that I can fix it. Why don't you put something else on and get washed up for dinner."

Magdalene was just so relieved that her mother wasn't angry with her that she completely forgot to tell her about the strange encounter she had with Mr. Remic.

Chapter 5

The winter of 1967 hit hard covering the Chicago land area with over twenty three inches of snow. Snowing nonstop from 5am Thursday morning stopping on Friday at 10am. The city was paralyzed, people abandoned their vehicles where ever they got stuck. Schools and business' were closed. Carl and Dorothy made sure that they had plenty of groceries, they knew the storm was coming. The kids jumped up and down cheering, "we don't have to go to school." Dorothy didn't mind, it was more time that she got to spend with her family. She was just concerned about Carl having to shovel all that snow.

After Dorothy put the kids to bed, her and Carl shared a romantic night together. Something they hadn't done since the surgery. Dorothy had feared that Carl wouldn't find her appealing anymore, but he quickly put her mind at ease. Falling asleep in each other's arms, Dorothy awoke when she heard a banging noise downstairs. Gently nudging Carl, she asked him, "did you hear that noise?" Just then there was another banging sound.

"I heard it that time," Carl replied. "I hope the furnace isn't gonna quit on us, not in this cold." Throwing on his robe, he slid his feet into his slippers to go down stairs to check.

"You can't go down there dressed like that, you'll freeze."

"I'll be fine. If there's a problem I'll come back up and get dressed."

Carl headed downstairs when he realized that Dorothy was right, it was freezing down there. Once he walked over to the furnace he could see that it was working just fine. Then he heard the banging again, but this time it appeared to be coming from somewhere behind him. With a chill running through him, he turned around to go back upstairs when he noticed that the door was closed. When he turned the knob the door wouldn't open, it was stuck. Using all his strength he yanked on the door trying to force it open, but it wouldn't budge. Suddenly, the basement lights went dim, and then went out.

Dorothy grew worried, it had been over fifteen minutes since Carl went downstairs. She knew how cold it could get down there. Putting on her robe, she went to check on him. Dorothy could hear the doorknob jiggling, she called out, "Carl are you okay?"

"The damn door is stuck, I can't get it open. Try and push on it from your side. It's freezing down here." Dorothy pushed and Carl pulled, but the door wouldn't open.

Magdalene woke up because she heard voices. Creeping down the hall she saw that the light in her parents room was on, but they weren't in there. Walking a little farther she noticed that the upstairs back door was open. As she stood there and listened she could hear her mother's voice. Magdalene walked down the first flight of stairs and called out, "Mommy is everything okay, where's Daddy?"

"Get back upstairs, it's freezing down here." No sooner did Dorothy say that when there was a click and the door opened. Carl hurried out, "everyone get upstairs, it's cold . Magdalene you get back to bed."

"I'll make you some hot cocoa, that should warm you up. Is the furnace okay?" Dorothy asked.

"Yah....it's fine. I'm not sure what was making that noise."

The weather started to break and things went back to normal. The kids went back to school and the stores were open for business. The harsh winter was fading and a beautiful Spring had begun.

Carl surprised the family when he announced, "for our summer vacation we're going to the Wisconsin Dells for a week." For the first time in eight months since Dorothy was diagnosed with cancer he finally started to believe she would be okay. Carl decided that it was time to start living again. After their trip to the Dells they went to the Riverview Amusement Park in Chicago before the kids started back to school. Magdalene thought that this had to be the best summer ever, and now it was coming to an end. "Mommy how come school is so long and summer is so short? I think it should be the other way around."

"Oh do you now," Dorothy replied with a chuckle.

Dorothy continued to help Philip with his homework and Magdalene with her reading, when she noticed that her vision was getting blurry, she also started getting headaches. Dorothy told herself, "it's just eye strain. I'm sure I just need a new pair of glasses."

As the weeks went by the headaches worsened. She was becoming easily irritated. One night in particular while Dorothy was helping Magdalene with her reading she had lost her place. Dorothy had warned her, "you had better start paying attention, I'm not in the mood for any nonsense.

"But Mom I really did lose my place."

All at once Dorothy picked up the belt that was laying on the table, swung it in the air and hit Magdalene in the eye. Grabbing her by the hair, Dorothy dragged her down the hall and threw her in the bedroom. Magdalene screamed in pain and lay on her bedroom floor crying, clutching the side of her face where the belt had struck.

Dorothy went back in the kitchen, sat down and prayed, "Dear God what have I just done to my little girl?" She was in tears when she picked up the phone and called Carl at work and told him that she needed him to come home, "it's an emergency." Without hesitation he left. Rushing through the back door, Carl saw Dorothy sitting at the kitchen table with her face buried in her hands. "What is it, what's worry?" Carl asked in a panic.

"I didn't mean it, for no reason at all, I just got so angry," Dorothy cried.

"Slow down and tell me what happened," Carl said trying to calm her.

Dorothy told him how angry she had gotten when Magdalene lost her place in the book that she was helping her read. She also told him how she swung the belt, hitting her little girl in the face. Carl stopped her and went down the hall to check on Magdalene. Now she just laid in bed quietly sobbing. He checked her face, then went and got her some ice to hold near her eye. Walking back in the kitchen Carl tried to calm Dorothy. She went on to tell him about the headaches and blurred vision. "I'm taking you to see Dr. Hall tomorrow, with or without an appointment," Carl said, holding back his anger.

When they arrived at the doctor's office, Carl told the nurse that they needed to see Dr. Hall right away, it was an emergency. He heard the commotion out in the waiting room and motioned for them to come in. Carl explained everything. Dr. Hall told Carl to take Dorothy to the hospital and he would call ahead so that they could have a room ready for her, he wanted to admit Dorothy and run some tests.

It wasn't long after the first set of tests were run when the doctor called Carl into a private office to tell him, "I have the results from the x-rays that we took," Dr. Hall told him. Taking a deep breath, he looked at Carl. "It's not good. The cancer metastasized, it's gone to her brain."

Carl exploded. "What the hell do you mean, it's gone to her brain. You told me that she was responding well to the treatment and that she was getting better."

"It happens that way sometimes. We remove the cancer from one area and it shows up in another."

"What am I suppose to tell her? How long is she going to be in the hospital this time?" Carl demanded answers.

"You don't understand, she's not going home. I'm sorry Carl, but she doesn't have much longer to live."

Carl collapsed back into the chair and just stared out the window, he was speechless. He could hear the doctor talking, but he just couldn't comprehend a word he was saying. "I want to have her moved to the sanitarium side of the hospital. They can care for her there, until the time comes." What was he going to tell Dorothy? What was he going to tell the kids?

They moved Dorothy to a private room in the sanitarium. Philip and Magdalene were too young to be allowed upstairs so they would bring Dorothy down to the solarium in a wheelchair to visit with them. They had no idea how sick their mother really was.

As Dorothy worsened the doctors would no longer allow her to go down to the solarium, but they did give Carl special permission to bring the children up to see her.

One night when Carl went up to visit Dorothy, she reached over and took his hand, "I'm worried about Philip, I know Magdalene can take care of herself, but I worry about Philip."

"He'll be just fine, you'll see." When Carl looked into her eyes, it was then that he realized that Dorothy knew she wasn't going home. He fought to hold back the tears.

The following week was worse. When Philip and Magdalene went up to visit with their mother, she looked different. Her skin had turned yellow, she shook, and couldn't stop coughing. The doctors told Carl that they couldn't allow the children to visit anymore. They also told him that it would be too hard for children that young to see their mother that way.

Carl had his mother watch the kids while he spent as much time with Dorothy as he could. Her sisters took turns visiting. Even under the circumstances her sister Sophie couldn't resist causing a scene.

Dorothy's lungs were filling up with fluid. Even though the doctors did what they could Sophie demanded that they do more. Dr. Hall pulled her aside , "we can only tap her so many times to draw the fluid out of her lungs. It's a painful process to run that needle through a person's back into their lung. We are keeping her as comfortable as possible. If you persist on causing a scene, you will not be allowed up here anymore," Dr. Hall firmly stated and walked away.

For once in her life Sophie actually didn't know what to say. It wasn't often people put her in her place.

The hospital allowed Carl to sleep in the chair in Dorothy's room at night. While her sister Helene was visiting, she wore a pin shaped like a flower on the lapel of her coat. Dorothy went hysterical, telling Helene that she had a big bug on her coat. Helene turned around and removed the pin and slid it into her coat pocket and told Dorothy, "it's okay, it's gone now."

Carl sat on the edge of the bed. Reaching out, he put his arms around Dorothy and held her. Looking at her as she struggled to breathe, he saw the once vibrant light that shined in her eyes start to fade. He leaned over kissing her on the lips and whispered in her ear, "we had a lot of good times together babe, and I'll never forget you." Carl held Dorothy a little while longer when he felt her let go.

Philip and Magdalene were watching TV while their grandmother was in the kitchen making lunch. Suddenly, Magdalene could sense her mother near her. Reaching over, she picked up a pad of paper and a pencil that was on the end table and wrote the words, Mom died. She handed it to Philip, as she looked over her shoulder to see her grandmother answer the phone. With a puzzled look on his face Philip asked, "how do you know?"

"I don't know," Magdalene replied. "I just know that she did." She refused to say it out loud. She was afraid that if she did, that would make it real. "I have to go outside and get some air." Magdalene got up off of the floor and headed for the front door.

"Where are you going?" Caroline asked.

"I just need to get some fresh air."

"I want to talk to you and Philip." Taking them both to the back porch they sat outside. Their grandmother wrapped her arms around them, and told them that their mother had died.

Part 2
It's Our Little Secret

Chapter 6

Dorothy was laid to rest April 7, 1968. She had died a few days after her 45th birthday and a week before Easter.

Carl tried to hold it together for his children. Even though he had known for some time that Dorothy didn't have much longer to live, it didn't make it any easier when the time came. Philip and Magdalene understood that their mother wasn't coming home anymore, they didn't quite realize the impact it would have on their lives.

It was Easter Sunday, Philip and Magdalene weren't sure with everything that just happened if the Easter Bunny would come. Carl felt that it was important to keep up with the family's traditions. After the kids went through their baskets they got ready to head into the city. It was their tradition to take the food that they would have for Easter dinner in a basket and have it blessed at St. Casmir's Church. Carl went through the motions in order to get through the day. He knew that things would never be the same.

With only two months left to the school year, Carl set out to find a house keeper. His foremen allowed Carl to go back to first shift under the circumstances. His mother tried to help as much as she could, but Caroline was in her late sixties and her health was deteriorating. Carl didn't think that she would be up to the challenge a nine year old girl and eleven year old boy could present. Unfortunately Carl wasn't having any luck finding a house keeper.

Dorothy's sister Mary called and asked if they could have some of Dorothy's personal things as a keepsake. Carl didn't see any problem with that, he would rather see her family get the clothes then strangers.

Early Saturday morning two of her sisters showed up with three of their friends. Carl was shocked, he couldn't believe how cold they were towards him. He watched them go through Dorothy's things like they were at a bargain basement sale on Maxwell Street.

After they picked through Dorothy's things her sister Sophie pulled Carl aside. "You had no right to hide the fact that my sister was dying, not from me or my family."

"I wasn't hiding it. I did what the doctor told me to do," Carl snapped back at her. "They felt that it would be better if she didn't know, and I knew you would have blurted something out with that big mouth of yours."

"You have no right talking to me like that," Sophie fired back.

"Look at all of you. Your pawing through all of her things like it's a feeding frenzy," Carl pointed out to her.

"Well just so you know, now that Dorothy's gone you don't count anymore," Sophie said, as she poked him in the shoulder.

After they left it was more than Carl could take. Reaching into the refrigerator he grabbed for a beer and cracked it open.

The kids were outside most of the day as Carl continued to drink, when Philip burst through the door and announced, "hey Dad, what's for dinner? It's almost six o'clock and I'm hungry."

Magdalene followed suit, " Yah, me too."

Carl muttered under his breath, "Shit....I forgot about dinner." He thought for a moment, then said, "come on, we're gonna go to the Westmont Lounge. I'll get you both cheeseburgers." He knew that he shouldn't be driving, he had way too much to drink.

Magdalene cheered, "I love their cheeseburgers."

"Me too," Philip added.

Carl's drinking steadily worsened. After he came home from work he took the kids to the restaurant for dinner and then came home, sat down at the kitchen table, and began drinking. He drank so much that he passed out. Magdalene and Philip were in the front room watching TV when Magdalene walked into the kitchen to get something to drink. Stopping quickly, she saw her father slumped over at the table. Becoming frightened, Magdalene ran back down the hall into the front room to get her brother. "I need you to come in the kitchen. I think that there's something wrong with Dad."

They both ran down the hall and just stared at their father."Is he dead?" Magdalene asked, trying not to cry.

"I don't know," Philip said, starting to tremble.

Standing there a little longer, Magdalene caught a glimpse of her father's chest heave in and out. "Look....I think I just saw him breathing."

"What do you think is wrong with him?" Philip asked.

"I don't know, he keeps drinking a lot of that beer," Magdalene said.

"Maybe he's just drunk," Philip replied.

It became an all too familiar sight in the months to come. Carl drank until he passed out at the table most every night. He started to miss work once or twice a week. Magdalene would wake up in the morning and sometimes see him at the table with his hand wrapped around a beer can and his head drooped forward as he began to pass out.

Maggie, which she now preferred to be called, spent most of her free time at her best friend Deena's house who lived two doors down. Maggie craved the life that she used to have. One with a mom and dad. Especially not with a father that got drunk, which was constantly now. Her brother didn't seem to be as effected by it like she was.

It was Saturday and they were headed out to the city for her cousin

Maryann's birthday. Maggie was thrilled, she hadn't seen any of her cousins since her mother died. Everything was going fine until Maggie noticed just how much her father was drinking, she hoped that he wouldn't do anything embarrassing. Although no one seemed to notice except her. They stayed most of the day, leaving before it got dark out.

Maggie didn't realize how drunk her father was until he started to drive. He had trouble keeping the car straight, he also slurred his words when he spoke. All of a sudden Maggie and her brother heard a horrible scrapping sound. They both started to scream. "You hit that car," Maggie yelled.

"Yah Dad, you just side swiped that car," Philip screamed.

"Stop....the both of you, shut up....you just shut your mouths," Carl said slurring his words. "I didn't hit anything....you hear me....I didn't hit a damn thing," he muttered.

The rest of the car ride was spent in silence. Maggie and her brother were afraid that they wouldn't make it home. Their father seemed to be driving a lot better, he had sobered up quite a bit after he had hit the other car. Pulling into the back yard, both of the kids breathed a sigh of relief.

Things got worse after that. One night in particular, they settled in to watch a Godzilla movie. Maggie had always loved scary movies. She slid under the end table that was next to the couch. This was something she did whenever they watched horror movies. It made her feel safe. Half way through the movie she felt something brush against her leg. Flinching, she moved over towards the wall, she thought that it might have been a bug. Then a little while later Maggie felt what appeared to be a hand moving up the inside of her leg. Looking up, she saw that it was her father. He was looking down at her.

Getting up, Maggie went and sat next to her brother in the chair. "Hey....why are you sitting next to me? There's not enough room," Philip complained.

"It's a scary movie," Maggie told him.

"Well go sit by Dad then," Philip said, nudging at her to go away.

Maggie refused to move. Luckily her brother was too involved in the movie to care anymore. After the movie Maggie went straight to her room and pretended to fall asleep. Sometime after midnight Maggie was awaken when she felt hands in a private place. When she could finally see through the darkness, Maggie realized that it was her father. "Shush....this is our little secret."

Maggie fought, she kept pushing his hands away. Begging for him to stop, she asked, "why are you doing this? Fathers aren't suppose to do things like this to their daughters," she kept pleading. "Deena's father doesn't do this to her." The truth was, Maggie really didn't know what happened in other people's homes. It seemed like forever, but her father finally got tired and staggered away.

This went on almost every night, sometimes during the day when Maggie's brother went outside to play. It got to the point that she would pray for her father to pass out at the table, just so he would leave her alone. When he did pass out, Maggie would go to Deena's house and stay as long as she could, sometimes spending the night. She was afraid to tell anyone what was happening to her. Even though she knew that it was wrong, Maggie didn't want the county to take her away. She remembered the orphanage that her parents took them to visit. Maggie told herself, "it would be worse to be alone with no family." So she kept her mouth shut.

Summer was almost over and school was starting in a couple of weeks. Maggie was thrilled. Anything that would keep her out of the house and away from her father made her happy. Although Maggie knew that she still loved her father, she didn't like what he had become.

It was harder then Maggie thought when she started the 4th grade. She felt that everyone was staring at her, that they knew that her father had been touching her. Maggie's school work suffered, any homework that she had, any tests that she was given, in the answer box she would just scribble. The answer wasn't even legible. This went on for months.

On the night of the parent teacher conference Carl managed to stay sober. Miss Franks the 4th grade teacher was a tall dark haired women. You could tell that most of her salary was spent on expensive clothes. There was nothing plain about her. She introduced herself and motioned for Carl to take a seat. "First of all I want you to know that Magdalene is a very sweet girl. She seems to be a bit introverted. I understand that you recently lost your wife, and I would like to say how sorry I am to hear that."

"Thank-you," Carl told her. "I appreciate that."

"I'd like to show you something," Miss Franks said, handing him a stack of papers.

"I can't read any of the handwriting on these papers," Carl said.

"Neither can we," Miss Franks told him. "I have to ask you Mr. Stanczyk, is everything alright at home?" Miss Franks questioned.

"I have to admit, it's been rough. I know Magdalene misses her mother a lot. I'm sure that's all it is. I'll talk to her when I get home," Carl told her. He felt the panic starting to rise inside of him. Thinking to himself, "what if they know."

They talked a while longer when Carl finally said that he needed to go. He made the excuse that the sitter he had needed to be home by a certain time. All he could really think of was how much he wanted a beer.

When he got home his brother was waiting for him. "Where are the kids?" Carl asked in a panic.

"I took them by Ma's house. I need to talk to you," Ray told him.

"About what?" Carl asked.

"Look....this is a small town and people talk. I work for the village and some of the people have been asking me a lot of questions about you and the kids."

"What kind of questions?" Carl asked. He could feel himself getting angry.

"Just hear me out. It's no secret that you've been drinking. When the police see you driving, they follow you home to make sure that you get there safe. They do that as a favor to me. They could throw you in jail. Your gonna lose those kids if you don't stop drinking." Ray shouted at him.

Carl slammed his fist on the table, *"no one is gonna take my kids, and I don't have a drinking problem. You need to leave."*

Ray knew better then to argue. Shaking his head, he looked at Carl and said, "I tell Ma the kids are spending the night with her." Ray turned and walked out the door.

Carl knew Ray was right, his drinking was out of control. He also knew there was something else he couldn't control. He needed to get Magdalene out of that house. Carl sat there thinking. He remembered that one summer Dorothy suggested sending her to camp O.L.B. He also remembered that during the school year Our Lady of Bethlehem was a boarding school. Next to that school was a Military Academy. "That would be perfect," Carl thought. He knew that it would probably cost more than he made, but the kids would be safe. He promised Dorothy that he would take care them. Carl couldn't let the county take them away.

Philip's grades weren't good enough for the Military Academy, but O.L.B accepted Maggie. Now came the hard part. Telling her she was going away. On the car ride there Maggie cried. She begged and pleaded for her father to change his mind. Her tears had no effect on him. His mind was made up.

Carl pulled up to the front door. Sister Fredrick the principle of the school came out to greet them. Maggie got out of the car with her suitcases. She barely had time to close the car door when her father drove off.

Part 3

High School, Séances, and Sunken Submarines

Chapter 7

Although Maggie had adjusted to a different life, in 1972 she was finally leaving the boarding school she had been in for the last three years. Now that she had graduated eighth grade, Maggie was going home to the friends she had left behind.

Her father wanted her to go to an all girls high school, but she had refused. Maggie liked boys, and the thought of going to Hinsdale South High School meant there were a lot of them. Maggie was excited and nervous. Her first class was algebra. She didn't recognize anyone in that class, but it was a big school. Maggie didn't expect to know everyone. She had a free period next so she went to the library and pretended to be interested in some of the books. Maggie was just killing time, she didn't have anyone to hang out with.

Maggie did think it was odd that her old friend Deena who lived two houses down from her didn't seem very friendly these days. The more that she thought about it she realized that it really didn't matter, she still had all of her other friends from the grade school she attended before her father sent her away.

Social studies was next. The teacher held the class in the theater were they actually taught drama. He felt that it would be more like a college atmosphere. He stood on stage and took roll call. Maggie heard him say the names of people she knew.

"Cindy Meyer"

"Here"

"Kevin Morris"

"Here"

"Jeff Hart"

"Present"

"Magdalene Stanczyk"

"Present"

All at once, most of the kids in the class turned and stared at her. The excitement Maggie had felt turned to panic and paranoia. She thought, "why are they just staring at me like that?" Then she wondered, why did they think she was sent away for three years? The feeling of horror set in twisting at her insides. Did they know what her father had been doing to her, did they think she liked it? If she wasn't the center of attention at that moment, she would have run out of there and never come back. Maybe an all girls high school wouldn't have been such a bad idea after all. Being homesick for her old friends may have clouded her judgment.

The days went from bad to worse, Maggie felt so isolated. Nobody really talked to her. The only class that she looked forward to was home economics. Maggie liked being creative, but that wasn't enough to keep her from ditching school.

Maggie was sitting on the floor in front of her locker, when a boy came up to her and said, "the war is over." Maggie looked at him and cocked her head, and he said, "the Vietnam war is over."

Maggie felt embarrassed because she didn't know much about it. In a catholic boarding school they didn't talk about war. They talked about God, and told you that everything was a sin. She smiled at him and nodded.

He stared at her for a minute and said, "I know you."

"You do?"

"Your Phil's little sister."

"Yes I am."

"I 'm Elliot, I thought I recognized you."

"I'm sorry I don't remember you, I've been away."

"Yah, your brother said you were in some special school or something."

"The way everyone is acting you would think I was in a loony bin, none of my old school friends will even talk to me. They just stare."

"Ah, fuck um then, you can hang out with me and my friends."

"Really?" Maggie said hopefully.

"Yah, come on."

"I'm only a freshmen."

"Don't worry about it, besides you don't look fourteen."

Maggie always looked older then she really was, which would prove to cause her problems later on. She followed Elliot down to the first floor and out the side door by the music rooms.

"This is where a lot of the juniors hang out," Elliot said. "This is Paul, Tommy, Max, Dove, and Llady......everyone this is Maggie."

"Wow, those are some cool names," Maggie replied.

"Well my parents were hippies," Dove said.

"Yah and mine, well I don't know what you would call my parents, they just liked the name Llady."

It made the school year a little easier having friends to talk to, but Maggie wasn't quite sure she really fit in. Even though she pretended to understand some of the things that they talked about.

She was hanging out with the gang when Max announced, "my parents are going away for the weekend so I'm planning on having a party. Everyone's invited."

"Hey Maggie you gonna go?" Elliot asked.

"I don't have any way to get there."

"I'll pick you up, I just got my license."

Maggie thought about it for a second and said, "yah sure I'll go." She smiled and thought to herself my first party. Maggie wasn't sure what to wear. She was sure that it wasn't anything fancy, so she put on her best pair of faded jeans and a peasant top. "Perfect," she said looking in the mirror.

Elliot got there about eight, Maggie didn't ask him in. Her father was passed out at the kitchen table drunk and she didn't want him to see that.

When they got to the party you could hear the music outside. It was one of her favorite songs, Eighteen, by Alice Cooper. When they walked in, Maggie sensed that she may be in over her head. She knew there would be drinking, but what she smelled in the air was not cigarette smoke.

Maggie opened a can of beer and slowly sipped it. She didn't want people to think she was a drag. They started to pass around a joint. Maggie watched what the others did and followed suit. They passed it around a few more times when Maggie started to feel twitchy, she wasn't sure if this was what it was like to be high.

She could hear In A Gadda Da Vida playing in the background when she noticed Tommy sitting in a chair looking back and forth at everyone. His eyes were darting everywhere as he kept rubbing his hands on the top of his pant legs.

"Is Tommy okay?" Maggie asked Elliot.

"Yah. He just dropped a hit of LSD, but it does look like he's getting a littleparanoid."

"Hey do you want another beer?" Elliot asked.

Maggie thought about for a second and said, "no, I'm good." She was afraid that someone might put something in it. Maggie didn't want to wind up like Tommy.

Another hour went by and Maggie decided that she wanted to go home, so she asked Elliot if he wouldn't mind taking her.

"Are ya sure you want to leave, it's still early?"

"Yah I'm sure."

Elliot agreed without an argument. Maggie wasn't sure if he said yes out of respect or that he realized she was only fourteen.

On the way to her house Elliot dropped hints to Maggie about inviting him in. She knew better. Maggie knew that she could never have company because her father was drunk most of the time, and she never knew what to expect from him.

He kissed her goodnight and was hoping for more when Maggie slid out of the car as fast as she could. She walked through the front porch door and stopped to dig for her keys when she looked up, and in the window of the front door she saw a face staring back at her. She screamed and backed up into the wall when she realized it was her own reflection in the glass, "you dumb ass," she said out loud panting, "stupid." Maggie went in, then she shut and locked the front door. The farther she walked into the living room she felt eyes on her. Maggie stopped, and when she turned around to look, the face in the window slowly disappeared. "Okay now you're losing it," she said under her breath.

Maggie tip toed down the hall to see if her father was still passed out at the table. He must have gotten up at some point and stumble to bed. She checked to see if he was still breathing, which is something she started to do after her mother died.

Maggie got ready to lay down. She was in bed laying on her stomach hugging her pillow, when she felt a hand on the back of her shoulder. She cringed thinking that it was her father, but when she turned around to look, no one was there.

As the weeks went by Maggie started to pull away from Elliot and the rest of the gang. She couldn't get the image of how Tommy acted at the party out of her head. She didn't want to wind up like that.

Elliot caught up to her in the hall and asked, "hey, you okay? We haven't seen much of you since the party."

"Yah, I'm fine. I haven't been doing so well in my classes, so I'm trying to make up for it. I've mainly been spending my free time in the library."

"That's cool, I guess you wouldn't want to be in high school for the rest of your life."

"Not hardly," she said laughing.

Maggie started ditching school more and more until she just stopped going all together in her freshmen year. She was surprised no one called the house to check on her.

During the summer Elliot stopped over from time to time using the excuse he was there to see her brother, but Maggie knew better. They never really hung out that much, and really didn't like the same things.

The following school year Maggie enrolled for her sophomore year, but never went.

Chapter 8

Now that Maggie was an official dropout she started to hang out with her cousin Terri. She was three years older and had a wild side. It really turned on the truckers that she often dated. Maggie's father didn't approve, but she felt that he really didn't have any right to judge.

Terri and Maggie had a lot in common. Her life was just as dysfunctional as Maggie's. Terri's step father would do things to her that he shouldn't. To him it didn't matter, daughter, stepdaughter, neighbor kid, he didn't discriminate.

Terri's mother had died a year before Maggie's did. It wasn't from cancer, her mother was hit by a car while walking home from work one night and left in a ditch. She died the next morning from her injuries.

Terri had a date with one of her favorite guys on Friday. Bill had a friend named Ronny that was, as he put it lonely, and asked Terri if she could hook him up with someone. She immediately offered up Maggie like she had done many times before. When Terri told her, Maggie let her know that she wasn't happy about it. After thinking it over, she decided to go anyway. Anything was better than being at home.

Bill came over Friday night to pick them up. There was a party going on at Ronny's house and Maggie was hoping that he was at least as cute as Bill. When they got there she realized why he was lonely. His hair was wild and frizzy and he had what Maggie would call summer teeth, some are here, some are there, not to mention his age, he had to be almost thirty. Maggie pulled Terri aside and asked her, "did you get a look at Bill's friend?"

"Oh relax, there's nothing wrong with him, he's fine," Terri said.

"If he's so fine why don't you date him!" Maggie snapped. She knew it was pointless to argue, she was stuck. All the people looked a lot older, except for one other girl that looked as miserable as Maggie. As soon as Ronny and the other guys went to go tap the keg, she went over to the other girl to introduce herself.

"Hi, I'm Magdalene, but I'd rather be called Maggie."

In a raspy voice, the other girl replied, "I'm Katelyn, but everybody calls me Kat."

"Is that your boyfriend ?" Maggie asked.

"Hell no! My friend couldn't make it so she dumped him on me. What about you?"

"My cousin wanted to go out with Bill and he had a friend. You know how that goes."

"Yah."

"I wish we could leave."

"Well I don't live to far from here. I know their talking about going downstairs to party. If we make up some excuse like we have to use the bathroom and wait for them to downstairs, we can sneak out the front door."

"The only problem is I don't have a car or a license," Maggie said.

"We can walk, I don't live that far."

Everyone started to go downstairs when Kat yelled out, "I'll be down in a minute, I have to use the bathroom." Maggie followed suit and said the same thing. They were the only two left upstairs.

"I think we should leave now," Kat said. "I bet your cousins gonna be pissed at you."

"She'll get over it."

As they walked they talked and got to know each other. Kat was the same age as Maggie. She also had dropped out of high school. Her parents were divorced, but her mother remarried.

"Hey you want to spend the night? My mom won't be home for quite awhile."

"She won't mind?"

"She's on one of her ghost hunting tours."

"Ghost hunting?" Maggie asked.

"Yah she goes on one almost every weekend. She's also studying to become a medium. She wants to start holding séances," Kat explained.

"That's so cool," Maggie said. "Do you believe in ghosts?"

"Yah, I think my grandfather visits a lot."

"Really," Maggie said. Then she thought, "finally someone that wouldn't think I'm crazy."

"I think my house is haunted, I've always heard weird noises, and once I felt someone touch me, but no one was there," Maggie went on to say.

"Wow, my mom would be interested in that."

They finally made it to Kat's house. Her younger sister was home watching TV. "Hey Leann, this is Maggie, and that's my sister Leann." They talked and played records until one in the morning, then decided to call it a night.

Kat's mother woke her up and enquired about who her new friend was. She explained to her that she was a friend of a friend and she was really nice. Kat's mother gave her the once over. By then Maggie woke up and said, "Hi I'm Maggie, it's nice to meet you."

"You can call me Lorraine," she told her.

"So how was your tour last night?" Kat asked.

"We went to Bachelors Grove"

"That's supposed to be one of the most haunted graveyards

around. I also heard the there's a farmhouse that will appear and disappear," Maggie said with a tone of excitement.

"Did you see anything?" Kat asked.

"We saw some orbs. Then over one of the headstones we saw a mist start to rise, but we didn't see any ghosts. I did take some dirt from one of the graves of a women that died in the mid 1800's. Tonight we're going to try and hold a séance. I want you, Leann and your friend Maggie to go to the roller rink for awhile."

"Why?"

"Because this is the first time we're trying this and I don't want you kids around. You have to be very careful when you're doing this. I don't want to invite anything evil into this house, so I don't need any distractions from you. Al can drop you kids off and he'll pick you up later."

As they were leaving for the roller rink Kat's Aunt Marie, Uncle Jim and Aunt Chris showed up for the séance.

After Al dropped them off neither Kat nor Leann knew that Maggie had no clue on how to roller skate. "If God wanted people to roller skate we would have all been born with wheels on the bottom of our feet," Maggie complained as she kept falling.

Back at the house Lorraine was getting everything ready for what they needed to have for the séance. She had put the dirt from the grave in the middle of the table next to the three candles. After everything was set Lorraine lit the candles and shut the lights off. Then the four of them sat down, held hands and closed their eyes. Lorraine told everyone to clear their minds as she started to concentrate and breathe deeply. She began to summon Mrs. Rodgers. That's what the name read that was on the headstone where Lorraine had gotten the dirt. Lorraine called to the women, beckoning to her, " make her presents known." After forty five minutes there was nothing. Lorraine was disappointed, but she vowed that they would try again.

"I'm gonna have Al pick up the girls. Help me put this stuff away."

When they got back to the house Kat and Maggie were curious about how things went. After noticing the look on her mother's face, they both decided that it might not be a good idea to ask. Kat told Maggie, "I think that it would be better if we just go in my room. I got some new records we can listen to."

Maggie's brother Phil picked her up Sunday night. She actually dreaded going home, but she knew she had too. Terri had called the house several times, and Maggie pleaded with her brother, "just tell her that I'm not home. *Please.*"

Maggie and Kat talked on the phone constantly. They were making plans for the upcoming weekend. Kat's mother was going on another ghost tour. They would have the house to themselves Saturday night.

Saturday afternoon Phil dropped Maggie off at Kat's house. When they went into her room she showed her a small bottle that had whiskey in it. She had taken it from her mother's bar.

"Won't she miss it?"

"Hell no, I put water in the bottle, that way it won't look like any is missing."

"Cool," Maggie said smiling.

They went in the living room to watch TV until her mother left. All of a sudden Maggie noticed the dog was just sitting there facing the wall, he appeared to be staring at it. "Why does your dog just sit there like that?"

Lincoln was a German Sheppard that Al had gotten from a friend that was a police officer. He was from the K-9 unit and was getting to old to keep up. "Lincoln always does that, it's like someone's petting him. He has been acting really weird this week though, kinda jumpy, and he looks like he keeps walking around something, only there's nothing there," Kat replied.

Kat's mother left at seven o'clock. Maggie put a stack of 45's on the stereo that they wanted to listen to, while Kat mixed the whiskey in some ginger ale. They started to dance when Kat stumbled and knocked over her drink. As she was walking towards the laundry room that was in the back of the house, she glanced in window of the back door and she saw the face of a hideous looking women behind her. She screamed so loud that Maggie jumped and Kat's sister came running out of the bedroom. By that time Kat was hysterical. "What is it?" Maggieasked in a frightened tone, "your scaring us."

"There was some one behind me, this ugly looking women."

"Kat there's no one here but us."

"Yes there is, I saw her. That's probably why Lincoln has been acting so weird."

"Okay, okay, I believe you. Let's just go in the living room and wait for your mom to get home."

"I'm not drunk you know. I know what I saw."

"I know, I believe you."

They huddled on the couch together until her mother came home. The minute she walked in the door Kat jumped up and ran towards her.

"Mom, I saw the face of a women behind me when I was going into the kitchen. She looked hideous, and so angry. Her face looked like it was decayed. What the hell was that I saw?"

"I don't know Katelyn, but I'm gonna try and find out," Lorraine said. "Why don't you girls go to bed. I'm home now, you'll be okay."

After they went into the bedroom Lorraine called Chris and told her what happened. "Maybe you did contact someone last weekend during the séance, and now that spirit is trapped in the house. They may not be able to find their way back," Chris suggested. Lorraine agreed and decided that she was going to have to call Mitch. He was a good friend of Lorraine and Chris. Mitch always organized the ghost tours. Lorraine knew that she was going to have to put the dirt back. She also knew he was going to be pissed.

Dialing the phone, the dread was starting to build. Lorraine needed Mitch's help and there was no way around it. When he answered the phone she immediately started to explain everything that occurred. Then she told him why she thought it happened. Just as she had thought, Mitch was passed angry, he was livid.

"I told you, I told all of you, not to touch anything. I told you to never disturb the dead, ever, they don't like it," he screamed.

"I know and I am so, so sorry," Lorraine cried.

"Do you remember where you took the dirt from?" Mitch asked.

"The name on the headstone was Mrs. Rodgers."

"The Madonna of Bachelors Grove," Mitch thought out loud.

"Who is that?"

"She's also known as the White Lady. She's sometimes seen in all white just sitting and staring out into the graveyard . She's buried next to her infant son. He died at birth and she followed him in death a week later. His loss was more than she could bear. Some people have said they've seen her holding a baby. When you took the dirt, you took something that belonged to her. It could have even belonged to her son. The lines get blurred over time, but she wants it back. We have to put it back tonight. If too much time goes by she won't be able to find her way back. I'll be there in twenty minutes," Mitch told her.

It was two in the morning. They had a half hour drive to the Bachelors Grove and a twenty minute walk through the woods to get to cemetery. They spent the car ride in silence. Lorraine knew that she had broken one of his most important rules, and he may not let her go on anymore tours. When they got there Mitch looked for a place to park were the police wouldn't spot the car, some of the local teens still went in the cemetery at night and partied. They had gotten about forty feet away from the entrance when Mitch grabbed Lorraine's arm.

"Shhhh, do you hear that?" Mitch whispered, "I hear footsteps."

"I hear voices, but I can't make out what their saying," Lorraine said.

"Come on let's hurry up and do this. Do you remember exactly where you got it from?"

"I think so."

"NO. You need to put it back exactly where you got it from."

Luckily Lorraine remembered exactly where she had gotten it from once they got there. They could still hear the rustling of leaves, and faint voices off in the distance. She put the dirt back down on the grave. They both felt a sudden chill go through them as they turned to hurry back to the car. As he drove Lorraine back home, Mitch told her that she should know within a week if the entity was gone.

Lorraine had decided not to go on anymore tours, she wanted to focus more on holding séances. She wanted to make sure that what happened with the Madonna of Bachelors Grove didn't happen again.

Chapter 9

The next few weeks went by and nothing else happened. The girls seemed to be okay. Lorraine was sure that the spirit of the White Lady was satisfied. Kat and Maggie were together constantly, they were either horseback riding, listening to records, or at the roller rink. They met a couple of boys that worked there, Brad was nineteen and liked Kat, Shawn was eighteen and liked Maggie. Kat was sure that her mother wouldn't approve if she knew, and she wasn't about to tell her. Lorraine and Al had planned to go up to Round Lake for the weekend, they had a cabin there, so Kat and Maggie made plans to go out with Brad and Shawn.

It was late afternoon when Lorraine said to Kat, "we're leaving and we won't be back until tomorrow, Leann is spending the night at Debbie's and I don't want you going out, and...."

"Mom!" Kat cut her off in mid sentence. "Why not?"

"I just don't want you going out, and I don't want any funny business, because I'll know if you do."

Kat was mad, after her mother left she told Maggie, "we're going out anyway."

"Are you sure about that?" Maggie asked. "Your mom seemed pretty definite about it."

"It's okay she'll never know, besides Brad and Shawn will be here at eight."

Kat informed Maggie that she was going to try something different with her hair and she wanted her to help her. She stood in the kitchen with her head in the sink washing her hair when she said to Maggie, "since you're standing right there can you please hand me the towel?" As Kat extended her arm back.

"Um, I'm sitting here at the table."

"You are?"

"Yep."

Kat pulled her head back out of the water and looked behind her, and there was no one there. "Wow I really thought that you were behind me."

Maggie helped Kat with her hair until she declared, "it's perfect, now all I need to do is put on my makeup and get dressed, and I'll be ready."

"Well I'm going to listen to some records while you're doing that," Maggie said.

Kat was in the bathroom using the mirror on the medicine cabinet to put on her makeup when it kept popping open, just enough to be annoying. She would shut it and a few minutes later it would pop open again.

Maggie yelled out from the living room to Kat, "have you seen my 45 Fox On The Run? I want to listen to it."

Just as Kat leaned back from the mirror to answer her, the cabinet door flew open with such a force, it missed Kat's face by inches before it slammed against the wall. Kat ran out of the bathroom and Maggie asked, "what the hell was that?"

Kat was frantic, "the medicine cabinet door flew open and almost hit me in the face."

"What do you mean, it just flew open?" Maggie asked.

"*Just what I said, it just flew open!*"

Just then the kitchen faucet turned on, then the bathroom sink, and finally the bathtub. At that point Kat and Maggie ran out the front door, refusing to go back in. They waited outside for Brad and Shawn to get there. Once they told them what happened neither one of them believed what they were being tell told. It didn't help when Brad went in the house and there was no water running anywhere.

"*What do you mean there's no water running, we're not making this up!*" Kat shouted.

"Well there's no water running now," Brad said . "Look..... this is just a little too weird, I think we're just gonna go."

"Fine , just go."

When Kat and Maggie went back into the house she called her mother and told her what happened.

"What were you doing?" Lorraine asked.

"Nothing," Kat said.

"*Katelyn, what were you doing?*"

"*Fine,* me and Maggie were gonna go out with some friends."

"Didn't I tell you not too?"

"Yah."

"Well don't worry, it won't hurt you."

"What won't hurt me?"

"Just behave, we'll be home tomorrow," Lorraine said as she hung up the phone.

Chapter 10

When Maggie's brother dropped her off at Kat's house Saturday afternoon, she had no idea what their plans were for the weekend. The minute she walked in the door Kat pulled her into the bedroom and told her that she had an idea.

"What is it?" Maggie asked.

"I found this ghost tour map in my mom's room and I've always wanted to go to Resurrection Cemetery to see where Resurrection Mary is buried," Kat explained.

"Yah but I thought nobody really knows who Mary is, most people say that she went dancing at the Oh Henry Ballroom in Willow Springs with her boyfriend when they had a fight and she left. Then she was supposed to have gotten hit by a car and left in a ditch. That was in the 1930's. Then there's another story that says her name is Ann, and she was killed around 1927, in some kind of car accident in Chicago. So how are we supposed to find her if we don't even know who she is?"

"Well it won't hurt to just look around the cemetery tonight."

"Tonight?" Maggie said

"Well yah, nobody ever sees her during the day," Kat said.

"How are we gonna get there?"

"I already have that figured out. We'll have Al drop us off at the roller rink tonight and then when he leaves we can walk to the cemetery, it's only four blocks away."

"What if we run into Brad or Shawn?"

"Don't worry we won't be in there that long, we'll go straight into the bathroom, wait a little bit and then leave."

Al agreed to take Kat and Maggie to the roller rink at seven o'clock. As they pulled up Kat let him know that she would call him when they were ready to come home. He sat there for a minute looking at her out of the corner of his eye.

"Why do you and mom always look at me like that?" Kat blurted out.

"Because we know you well enough to know that most of the time you're up to something."

"We're not up to anything, we're just going roller skating."

"Alright, just give me a call when you're ready to come home."

They both went into the roller rink and hurried into the bathroom so they wouldn't run into Brad or Shawn. They sat in the locker room until eight o'clock, they thought it would be better if it was dark outside. Kat thought that they could sneak in, she heard that there was some kind of gap in the bars of the fence. Maybe it would be big enough for them to squeeze through.

They left the bathroom and hurried out the front door. As they were walking to the cemetery they both started to wonder, what would they do if they actually saw the ghost of Resurrection Mary. As they approached the cemetery Kat found the section of bars that was pushed in. "Here," she said. "They say that something evil was trying to get out one night and that's why the bars are bent.".

"Kat," Maggie said. "If they were trying to get out the bars would be pushed out not in. I think a car hit the fence."

"Well, okay that makes sense, I guess, but there is a part of the fence that has burn marks on it, and it's in the same place that people have sworn they saw her walk through the bars."

Both Kat and Maggie were able to squeeze through the fence. The map they had was very vague, in reality no one really knew where in the cemetery Mary's body was buried, if she was there at all. The legend is, she's either seen hitch hiking by the cemetery wearing the white dress she was killed in, or the men that have picked her up say that when they drive by the cemetery she tells them to stop and she jumps out of the car and runs through the gates and disappears.

Kat and Maggie were determined to find her. They wore dark clothes in hopes that they wouldn't be seen. They walked along the fence looking for the section that was burnt, they thought that if they found it, that would be a good place to start. They walked around for a half an hour when Kat got excited and could barely speak, "Maggie, Maggie, look, look, that's it, the burn marks on the fence."

Maggie stood there and stared in disbelief, "your right they are burn marks."

"I told you," Kat screeched.

"Okay, now which way do we go?" Maggie asked.

"Let's go this way, if she was running in, maybe she was going in that direction."

As they walked farther in they noticed that they were in a more secluded part of the cemetery, not well lit and away from the roads that went through. Resurrection Cemetery was laid out in a triangular pattern, Archer Ave flanked one side and 79th St. flanked the other side. Kat and Maggie had lost track of how long they had walked. They were in the middle of the cemetery towards the back. It looked like they were in an older section. "Look at some of the dates on these headstones, some of them are from the late 1800's and early 1900's, so we must be in the right spot," Kat said.

"Something doesn't feel right, it feels like someone is watching us," Maggie said as she looked all around.

"Nobody knows that we're here," Kat told her.

Just as Kat said that, Maggie pointed towards the cluster of trees, "I see eyes, orange eyes, at least six of them, and their headed right for us."

"Oh shit, run," Kat shouted. "Come on, this way."

They both started running, weaving in and out through the head-stones as they kept looking over their shoulders. The orange eyes were getting closer. All of a sudden Maggie heard a scream and froze in her tracks as she though, "they got her, they got Kat." She was paralyzed with fear. Maggie wanted to turn around and look, but she was afraid of what she would see. Just then, she thought that she felt something touch the back of her neck as chills ran down her spine.

A minute or two had pasted, although it felt like a life time in Maggie's mind, when she heard Kat calling her name saying, "help me Maggie, help me." She turned around and saw that the orange eyes were gone, and so was Kat. She called out, her voice trembling, "Kat where are you?" She waited for a response, and then she heard, "I'm down here, I fell in a hole." Maggie stepped carefully so she didn't fall in the same hole, "keep talking so I can follow your voice."

"I'm here, I'm right here," Kat kept saying. When Maggie found her, she noticed that the hole she had fallen in was a fresh dug grave. "Kat you fell in a grave."

Kat cried, "get me the hell out of here." Maggie told her she didn't know if she was strong enough to pull her out. When Maggie looked up she saw a light bouncing around in the distance, "Kat I see a light and it's coming straight towards us." Maggie instructed her to keep her back against the side of the grave so she wouldn't be seen and she was going to hide behind the mausoleum. "Just be quiet, okay."

"I'm scared," Kat said as Maggie disappeared.

What seemed like forever was only a few minutes. Kat could here twigs snapping and leaves rustling as she held her breath. She could hear a faint voice say, "is anybody there, I heard a scream, do you need help?" Kat recognized the voice, it was Mitch her mother's friend. Kat yelled, "I'm down here, I fell in a grave, help me." By that time Maggie came out of hiding when she heard Kat's voice.

"Mitch, what are you doing here?"

"My question is, what are you two doing here?"

"We need to get Kat out of there. Please." Maggie begged.

Mitch was able to lift Kat out of the grave easily. Luckily enough she wasn't hurt, just a little dirty. Then he looked at the both of them and told them that they had some explaining to do. They told him about finding the tour map and that they wanted to see if Resurrection Mary would appear. They also told him about being chased by the orange eyes. Mitch informed them, "the orange eyes were coyotes and when Kat screamed that was enough to scare them away."

"Okay," Kat said. "You know why we're here, now, why are you here?"

"Since it's getting close to Halloween one of my biggest tours is tomorrow, people want to see ghosts, people expect to see ghosts, so sometimes I come here at night and put certain items around so people think that she's been here."

"So Mary is a fake?" Maggie asked.

"No the legend of Resurrection Mary has been around longer then I've been alive. There has been people that have seen her, but you can't make spirits perform for you on command. So I help it along sometimes," Mitch said. "Come on I'll take you home."

"Can you take us to the roller rink instead? That's where Al thinks we are."

"Sure, I'll keep your secret if you keep mine."

"Deal."

They got back to the roller rink at quarter to eleven and hurried into the bathroom. Kat cleaned herself up the best that she could and then called Al and let him know that they were ready to come home.

When Kat awoke the next morning she could hardly move, falling in that grave was worse than being thrown from a horse, which she had experienced a few times. The good thing was that neither her mother or Al seemed to suspect what her and Maggie had been up to the night before. Kat felt so bad that she told Maggie that she didn't feel up to going out. They had plans to go to the stables for a haunted horseback ride. The stable owners always held a Halloween themed event throughout the month of October. The woods and the trails were decorated with hanging corpses, and a witch's cottage with a caldron and a screaming ghoul being boiled in oil. There would also be someone dressed as the werewolf ready to jump out at people riding on the trails in the evening. After the trails were closed there was a costume party in the main stable, Kat was going as a pirate and Maggie was going to be a black cat.

"Why don't you go without me," Kat relented. "I feel horrible."

"It wouldn't be the same without you," Maggie said.

"Hey, I have an idea," Kat's tone perked up. "We can have a party here, you me, and Leann. I think I can sneak some of my mom's booze from the bar, and we can get hammered while we watch horror flicks."

"I can go for that," Maggie liked the idea. She loved horror movies and she didn't mind staying in after last night.

Just then Kat's mother came through the bedroom door wanting to know what time they were going out.

"We're not going out. I don't feel good," Kat informed her.

"*What do you mean you're not going out?*"

"*What's the big deal? Half the time you don't want me to go out.*"

" If you must know I'm having company tonight."

"*So.*"

"*Katelyn.*"

"*What?*"

"We're having a big séance tonight and I don't want you to interrupt us." Lorraine was just worried that if anything went wrong she didn't want the girls around. She didn't want anyone getting hurt.

"I promise, we won't bother you. I really don't feel good."

Lorraine thought about it and decided that she must be telling the truth, because she knew that Katelyn would never pass up the opportunity to go out.

Chapter 11

Lorraine's friends started to show up around nine thirty. This was Al's cue to head down the street to the corner bar for a few beers, he always like to stay close just in case Lorraine had any problems. He loved and respected her passion for the paranormal even though he didn't participate in any of it himself. Al would always tease her and ask, "who's spirit do you plan on chit chatting with tonight?"

Lorraine felt that she was stronger now as a medium, she had learned how to channel her energy and stay focused during a séance. They started to hold them closer to midnight. The group would say a prayer before they started to keep any negative energy away. The table was set with three candles , Lorraine also put a glass of water in the center of the table that she would use when she asked the spirits to show themselves. If they were present sometimes you could see ripples go through the water. A tape recorder was set on the counter, the group would play it back to see if it had picked up any types of noises that they couldn't hear during the séance.

Tonight they were going to try to contact Lorraine's Uncle Ed who was in WWII. All any of them knew about him was that he died in combat, Ed was Lorraine's father's brother. She had heard from her Aunt Marie that her mother was dating George, but when she met Ed it was love at first sight, so she dated him behind George's back.

Louise, Lorraine's mother knew that Ed was leaving to go overseas to fight in the war. They both vowed that when he came home they would tell George so that she could end the relationship with him, and then Louise would be free to marry Ed, but neither of them knew that Ed was never going to come home. All that anyone really knew was that he died in combat. What Louise didn't know was that George already knew about her relationship with Ed, but he loved her unconditionally and still married her even though he had always wondered if Lorraine was really his or Ed's daughter.

The table was set and all they needed now was the picture of Ed that Aunt Marie had, it was the only one that existed, Louise had no idea that Marie had it. Louise also didn't know that Marie had a brief affair with Ed before he went overseas.

The picture was placed in the circle between the candles so that Lorraine could focus her energy on it. She lit the candles and turned on the tape recorder, then turned the lights off. Lorraine started to breathe deeply, she channeled all of her energy on the picture of Ed, they held hands and closed their eyes. She invited Ed into the circle. "Send us a sign. Let us know if you can hear me," she implored him to make his presents known.

At first the water in the glass rippled and then nothing. Lorraine began to focus harder, she continued to call out to him, she demanded he make his presents known. She could feel something, she could feel a presents. The air felt thick and heavy, the glass started to vibrate and the water started to bubble, then all at once there was a boom, it felt like the whole house shook. Lorraine and the others were careful not to let go of each other hands, they did not want to break the chain.

Maggie watched as Kat stared at the bedroom door wide eyed. "I know you heard that . What do you think we should do?." Maggie whispered.

"I don't know, if we go out there and there's nothing wrong we'll ruin their séance and my mom will be pissed," Kat warned.

"How can there not be anything wrong, my God you heard that. It sounded like something exploded," Maggie said.

"I'm sure everything's okay, I'll just listen at the door just to make sure," Kat assured Maggie.

Lorraine kept urging Ed to communicate with her, "tell me what happened to you, how did you die?" They heard what sounded like the water glass crack, all at once water started to seep out of the crack. Lorraine started to sound like she was having a hard time breathing, but she wouldn't let up, she kept probing and pleading with Ed to tell them what had happened to him. As soon as Lorraine asked that question water started to spray out of the faucet. Everyone had noticed that it was getting harder for Lorraine to speak. It was becoming more difficult for her to breathe. She kept pushing the question. The water now started to gush out of the faucet, then all of a sudden Lorraine let go of the hands that she was holding and grabbed for her chest gasping for air. Her brother Jim ran to her side rubbing her back coaching her to breathe. Aunt Marie blew out the candles, took the picture and put it face down and then turned on the lights to disconnect all spiritual energy. The faucet had stopped spraying water and there didn't seem to be a crack in the glass, although you could see a small puddle of water around it. Ten minutes had gone by when Lorraine started to breathe normally.

"Are you okay?" Jim asked, still shaken by the events that just happened.

"I felt like I was suffocating, there was so much pressure surrounding me. I felt like the life was being squeezed out of me, there was just so much pressure."

"But, are you okay now?" Jim persisted.

"Yes, I'm okay now."

Kat and Maggie burst out of the bedroom, Kat couldn't take it any longer not knowing what was happening to her mother.

"Mom," she shouted. "Are you okay?"

"Katelyn, you and Maggie go back in your room, I'm fine."

"*No, I will not go back in my room, what just happened out here?*"

"We heard that horrible boom. It shook the whole house and then we could tell you couldn't breathe," Maggie said, still shaken by what they heard.

"To be honest with you, I really don't know what happened. Water started spraying everywhere and then I couldn't breathe."

"Did anyone listen to the tape to see if maybe you could hear anything strange?" Maggie suggested. Everyone just stood there and looked at each other as if to say, "the tape recorder."

"With everything that just happened I completely forgot about the tape recorder," Lorraine said.

They rewound the tape to the beginning and started to listen to it. At first you heard them pray, then you heard Lorraine asking for Ed to show his presents. Then for a long while you heard nothing other than her questions. Further into the recording you could hear what sounded like pinging.

Kat spoke up, "what is that?"

"*SSSH*, be quiet," Lorraine snapped.

They continued to listen. They began to hear faint voices, a man, it sounded like he said, "*send an SOS.*" Another man replied, "*yes Captain.*"

The longer they listened, chills began to run down their spines. At that point the noise in the background became more defined, it almost sounded like steel being compressed. They could now hear the voices of the other men begin to panic. You heard a voice say "water is seeping in, the seams can't take any more pressure Captain." You could clearly tell the voices on the tape were becoming more strained. "The pressure is too much," for what sounded like he said the Saint Lorraine.

The sounds started to become more intense, steel fracturing, rivets popping, men screaming, Saint Lorraine, over and over again, and then silence.

Kat stood there trembling. Maggie had tears in her eyes as she whispered, "those poor men."

"What do you think happened to them?" Kat asked.

Lorraine just sat there shaking her head and said, "I don't know."

They listened to the tape over and over again for the next hour, and each time they heard something new that they hadn't heard the time before.

Lorraine wondered if any of the voices that they heard could have belonged to her Uncle Ed. She had never known him since he died before she was born, so she had no way of knowing what he sounded like. Her Aunt Marie just couldn't be sure if any of the voices might have belonged him. It was so long ago when she last spoke to him.

Lorraine looked at Jim and asked, "what did that sound like to you?"

"Well, when I was in the Navy I spent my time on a destroyer, but it actually sounded like noises that you would hear on a submarine. Some of the guys that were on the subs said that if you went to deep the pressure would cause the steel to groan and creak. I've even heard that too much pressure can cause a sub to implode. Although, I don't know of any that have," Jim replied.

"Do you think that's what happened to those men? Maybe something hit the submarine and it started to sink, and then it imploded from the pressure?" Lorraine asked, searching for an answer. She had so many thoughts and question running through her mind. Was that what happened to her Uncle Ed? "Jim, do you think that Uncle Ed could have been on the Saint Lorraine?"

Jim thought out loud, "I don't think there was ever any subs named the Saint Lorraine. They didn't generally name subs after women. Officially they were either named after fish or they were issued some type of USS numbers, not unless it was some sort of nick name given to her by the crew."

Maggie chimed in, "I don't think that they were saying Saint Lorraine

. The more I listened to the tape, it actually sounded like they were saying save us Lorraine." Just then another chill ran down everyone's spine.

When they played the tape again they realize that Maggie was right, the men were franticly screaming, "save us Lorraine, save us."

"*Mom*", Kat blurted out. "You have to do something with this tape. You have to tell someone about it. This is proof that you *can* communicate with the other side."

Lorraine thought about it for a moment and then said, "I wouldn't even know where to take it."

Chris spoke up, "why don't you get a hold of Mitch, he runs all those haunted tours maybe he knows of a group that can help you do some sort of research about the sub and the men on it."

The minute Chris said Mitch, Kat and Maggie looked at each other with the look of panic on their faces. They both were afraid that if Lorraine talked to Mitch, he would tell her about what happened the night before. Unfortunately Lorraine caught the look that the girls gave to each other, narrowing her eyes she said, "*what was that look about Katelyn?*"

"*What look?*"

"*I saw the look you and Maggie gave each other.*"

"*Mom,* there was no look, okay, but do you think Mitch is the best choice?" Kat actually started to wonder how legit he really was.

"What do mean is he the best choice? Mitch knows a lot about these things."

Before Lorraine could say another word Kat and Maggie hurried back into the bedroom.

"I heard everything that was said out there, do you think that Mitch will tell mom about last night?" Leann asked.

"I hope not, but if he tells her about last night, we can tell her what he's been doing," Kat said. "I'm just starting to wonder how legit he really is," she added.

"We'll just have to wait and see," Maggie interjected.

Chapter 12

Lorraine could hardly sleep, she had so many unanswered questions running through her mind.

When morning finally came she called Mitch and asked him to come by, she needed to talk to him. Mitch seemed nervous, but he agreed. He wasn't sure if Katelyn had mentioned anything to her mother about the night before, but there was only one way to find that out. Mitch got there not knowing what to expect, but he decided to go in as if nothing was wrong.

Kat and Maggie went to the stables, they wanted to make sure they were gone before he got there.

Lorraine greeted him at the door, her mind was racing and she couldn't stop talking. That put Mitch at ease, because it didn't sound like she was talking about the events that happened at the cemetery with the girls, although he had no idea exactly what she was talking about. Mitch took her by the arm and made her sit down and told her, "you need to slow down, I can't understand a word your saying."

"Okay," Lorraine took a deep breath and continued slowly. "Last night we had a séance. We were trying to contact my Uncle Ed. He died in WWII before I was born."

"Okay, what happened?"

"Well, we recorded the séance in case there was something we missed or maybe we couldn't hear. Look.... I think it would just be easier if I play the tape for you instead of me trying to explain it to you," Lorraine told him.

Mitch couldn't believe what he was hearing, he sat there stunned. When the tape finished he asked if he could listen to it one more time. Lorraine could tell by the expression on Mitch's face that even with all his paranormal experience he had never heard anything like that before.

After they listened to it the second time, Lorraine said, "this is why I called you, I want to share this tape. I want people to know that you can communicate with people that have crossed over, but I don't know if there are any experts in this kind of thing. I know that they would probably have to verify the tape first."

Before she could finish, Mitch cut her off and started to ramble on. "Do you realize how much money we could get for something like this, how famous we could be with this kind of proof."

"Hey....now wait just a minute," Lorraine cut him off. "This isn't about getting rich, this is about proving to the world that you can contact the dead."

"Your right, I apologize, you are absolutely right," Mitch's tone changed. "I know of several paranormal societies that may be able to help us with this. Why don't you give me the tape. I know of one place in particular that is also very reputable and since they know me, I think that they'll be able to help."

"Really? Do you really think so?" Lorraine needed to be reassured.

"Definitely," Mitch said. "I'll go straight there after I leave here."

She handed him the tape and told him, "please be very careful with this, that may be all I have of my Uncle Ed."

"I will," Mitch said. "You can trust me," he told her as he left.

Lorraine was hopeful, but after awhile something started to gnaw at her. She pictured Mitch's face, how the look of greed started to take over when he was talking. Since Mitch said that he was going to the Paranormal Society when he left, she hoped that she would hear from him later that night.

Chapter 13

Kat and Maggie had stayed out a little later than usual. One of the guys brought a couple of twelve packs of Old Style. They both decided to stay and party with the gang for awhile. Kat sat down and kicked her feet up on a bale of hay and declared, "after the past couple of nights that I've had, I could use a beer or two."

"I agree," Maggie laughed.

They got home a little after one in the morning. Every light in the house was off. They both thought that they had escaped the wrath of Lorraine. She would have come down on the both of them for staying out so late. They tip toed to the bedroom. All of a sudden from out of the darkness they heard, "it's after one in the morning Katelyn, *and* I smell alcohol. Where were you two?"

They both froze in their tracks. Then Kat blurted out, "*Mom.....* you scared the shit out of us. What are you doing up so late? Not to mention sitting in the dark."

"You first."

"We were hanging out at the stables with some friends."

"And?"

"Okay one of the guys brought some beer, so we had a few."

"You two aren't old enough."

Kat thought something was wrong, because the real Lorraine

would have screamed them both stupid, not just for staying out so late but for drinking. Kat sat down. "Mom what's wrong? Your just sitting here in the dark. Did something happen with Mitch?"

"I think that I may have made a big mistake."

"Why what happened?" Maggie asked as she eased to the kitchen chair.

"I played the tape for Mitch. I asked him if he knew of a place that I could take it too. He said that he did know of someplace."

"And?" Kat prodded.

"Well....after we listened to the tape a couple of times, he got this look in his eyes and stated to say how rich and famous we could be with this kind of proof."

"We... he had nothing to do with this," Kat snorted, as she raised her voice.

"Then what happened?" Maggie asked.

"He apologized and said he knew of a place he could take it."

"Please tell me that you didn't give him that tape."

The look on Lorraine's face said it all.

"Mom....please tell me that you at least make a copy."

Lorraine just looked at her daughter and shook her head no.

"Oh Mom."

"I tried calling him. I thought that maybe I would have heard from him by now. He's not answering his phone."

"Look.... why don't you just give it a couple of days. He might just need a little time to talk to these people," Maggie said. Hoping that would make Lorraine feel a little better.

"Yah," Kat agreed. "We should all just go to bed. You'll feel better in the morning Mom, you'll see."

"All right." Lorraine knew that there wasn't anything else that she could do about it , except wait.

When they went into the bedroom Maggie said, "we should have told your mom that Mitch wasn't exactly honest about his supernatural business. If she knew that ahead of time she might not have given him the tape."

"I know, but we can't tell her now. She'd be so pissed there is no telling what she'd do. That tape meant everything to her. That could have been her Uncle Ed's voice on it."

"What are we gonna do Kat? I hate seeing her like this."

"I know, but there's nothing we can do about it now. Let's just get some sleep."

Chapter 14

Over a week went by and Mitch still hadn't called Lorraine. When she tried to call him, there was either no answer or the line was constantly busy. More like it was off the hook. Lorraine felt as if Mitch, someone that she had known for so long had betrayed her.

At this point she was more angry with herself. She was usually so good at reading people and situations. This time Lorraine had to admit to herself that she made a huge mistake by giving Mitch the tape.

How many decades people have claimed that they can communicate with the spirit world, and how many times has it been proven to be a hoax? This time she had proof and it was real. She was just so desperate to show the world that it is real, she left herself vulnerable.

Lorraine wouldn't stop beating herself up. She should have never let him leave with that tape. Another three weeks went by, Lorraine was livid. She hadn't heard a word from Mitch. As a matter of fact a lot of the same people they knew were starting to avoid her. Even the girls had made themselves scarce. She had been snapping at everyone that came within ten feet of her.

This was the last phone call she was going to make. If Mitch didn't answer, Lorraine decided that something else needed to be done. She slammed the phone down and turned around to find Chris standing there. "You scared the shit out of me," Lorraine snapped as she stumbled backwards into the stove. "What are you doing here Chris?"

"I heard something the other day and you're not going to like it," Chris replied. "I was talking to one of Mitch's friends. I don't think that they realized that we're friends, let alone that I was at the séance that night."

"Okay.....and?"

"He took your tape to some institute that deals with that type of thing. He told them that he recorded the séance that night."

"He what?" Lorraine cut Chris off before she could say another word. "My voice was on that tape not his."

"They don't care about who lead the séance. They were just fascinated with the contents on the tape. They offered Mitch a lot of money for it."

"Son of a bitch," Lorraine bellowed. "Come on, let's go."

"Where are we going?" Chris asked. Becoming nervous and afraid of finding out the answer to that question. She had never seen Lorraine that angry.

"We're gonna take a ride to Mitch's place."

"Do you really think that's a good idea? He won't answer the phone. What makes you think the he'll answer the door."

"It won't hurt to try," Lorraine snapped.

Chris had a sick feeling in the pit of her stomach. There wasn't anything good that was going to come out of visiting Mitch, she thought.

When they got there Chris parked a few houses down. Lorraine did not want to give him any warning to their arrival. As they approached the front door Lorraine thought that she heard the TV. As soon as she rang the door bell everything went silent. At this point Lorraine was irate. She began banging on the door screaming, "I know that your home Mitch. Open the door."

The screaming and banging got louder. Chris couldn't take it any longer. Grabbing Lorraine's arm, she spun her around and screamed. "Stop it, just stop it. He isn't going to answer the door. You screwed up. You should have never given him that tape. There's nothing that you can do about it now. Let's just go before someone calls the police."

Lorraine stood there stunned, Chris had never spoken to her like that before. She realized that there was nothing anyone could do about it now. The tape was gone. Walking back to the car they heard someone ask, "is everything alright Ladies?"

When they turned around there was a police officer standing behind them. "We got a report that there was loud screaming and a possible fight. Is there a problem?"

"No officer, it was just a misunderstanding." Lorraine chose not to explain any further. Actually, she felt that he might think the both of them were insane if she did.

The two drove in silence on the way back to Lorraine's house. When she got out of the car Chris drove off not wanting to go in. Al was standing in the kitchen. He had his car keys in his hand. "Are you going somewhere?" Lorraine already knew the answer to that. No one wanted to be anywhere around her. Ever since this whole thing started between Mitch and her, Lorraine had been miserable. The girls went out every chance they got. Al went up the street to the bar as often as he could. Pulling out a chair to sit down Lorraine told Al, "I need to talk to you."

"What is it Hun?"

After explaining what had happened at Mitch's house, Lorraine looked at Al and said, "I owe you an apology. I've been acting like an ass."

"Well....I'm glad you said it before I had to tell you." Al just leaned back in his chair. His big belly giggling as he chuckled.

"I'm going to apologize to the girls when they get home," she said, trying to force a smile.

"That's my girl," Al said as he got up. Walking over to her, he slapped her on the behind and told her, "I'll see you later babe."

There was a burst of laughter as the front door opened. The girls were talking about the fun they had at the stables. Lorraine called out from the kitchen. "I need to talk to the three of you."

Cringing, they walked into the kitchen and sat down. After an hour had gone by they were talking and laughing as if nothing had happened.

"Mom we've been thinking. Why don't you have another séance? Maybe you can contact those men again," Kat suggested.

These things rarely happen the same way twice," Lorraine warned.

"Well......it wouldn't hurt to try," Maggie gently nudged towards the idea.

Being out numbered, Lorraine surrendered. "Okay, I'll think about it. You three go to bed. It's getting late."

The truth was, no one really wanted her to hold any more séances. Kat was just trying to humor her mother. She wanted things to go back to the way that they used to be.

The tension and negativity had eased. Things seemed to be returning to normal. Lorraine felt that she had finally gotten control over her anger and hostility towards Mitch. Accepting the fact that she would never be able to get the tape back again, would it be risky to try another séance? Sometimes when you want something so badly you can accidentally open a door to something evil, Lorraine mused.

The phone rang breaking her concentration. Chris was anxious. She kept repeating over and over, "answer the phone, come on pick up the phone."

Not knowing who to expect on the other end, Lorraine walked over to the phone and answered it. Chris blurted out, "it's about time," before she really knew who was on the other end.

"What do you mean, it's about time?" Lorraine was used to Chris's outbursts. There were times that she considered Chris to be over dramatic.

Not being able to contain herself any longer. Chris came right out and said it. "Mitch is dead."

There was a long silence. Chris waited for Lorraine to absorb the news before speaking again. When there was no response, Chris spoke up, "did you hear what I said?"

It was another few minutes before Lorraine spoke, clearly shaken by the news. "What happened?"

"They're not really sure. They think he may have had a heart attack."

"A heart attack, what actually happened? Who told you this?" The questions kept coming.

"I spoke to a friend of his. He told me that Mitch was going to meet some people. I think it had something to do with the tape. That was two nights ago. They said that he never showed up. One of Mitch's friends went to his house and saw that his car was in the driveway, but he wasn't answering the door. When he looked through the window he could see him sitting at the dining room table. He wasn't moving. His friend went over to one of the neighbors and called the police."

"How did they get in?"

"They had to break in. Now this is the scary part. They said he was sitting at the table just staring, his eyes wide open. It was almost like he had seen a ghost. His friend said that he was clutching something in his hand. Whatever it was, was burnt and melted onto his skin. They don't think that they'll be able to remove it. It's fused to his hand."

"Do you think that it was the tape?" Lorraine asked. Her voice trembling.

"I don't know," Chris sighed.

After another long silence, Lorraine's last thought was out loud. "He wanted that tape so bad. Now he'll never be able to let it go."

Part 4
The Final Séance

Chapter 15

It was already two weeks into the new year. Lorraine had missed the holidays. There was no one to blame but herself, she thought. All that time spent obsessed over Mitch taking the tape. Lorraine realized how funny that sounded to keep telling herself that he took the tape when she had just handed it over to him without hesitation. She didn't even make a copy. Then there was his sudden death. Sometimes she could still feel a slight anger wanting to resurface.

No one in Lorraine's family or circle of friends other then Chris knew that Mitch was gone. They both decided to keep it that way. He had no family and there was nothing in the news about his death let alone that it may have been suspicious. If Al were to find out he would never allow her to have another séance. If the truth were to be told, that was exactly what she was planning on doing, holding another séance.

Lorraine had struggled with that decision. In the short time she had spent obsessing over Mitch, so many things had changed at home. The girls seemed to have grown up overnight. Katelyn was dating someone. All she knew about him was that his name was Randy, but everyone called him Smoke. Leanne and Maggie had become close, somewhat inseparable. There didn't seem to be any more questions about the tape. Everyone seemed to have moved on with their lives. Lorraine just wasn't ready to let it go yet, she couldn't.

Lorraine and Chris went to the library . They wanted to do some research on submarines that may have sunk in WWII. She wanted to focus on contacting the same men whose voices were on the tape. She thought that it would help if they could pin point a time frame of when the submarine may have sunk. None of the information that she read sounded familiar. Nothing matched up with what they heard on the tape that night. Lorraine knew she was going to have to duplicate the events of that night from memory.

Now came the hard part, telling Al what she was planning. Just as Lorraine sat there contemplating how to tell him, her concentration was broken. She didn't hear him come through the back door.

"You seem to be in deep thought, judging by the way you jumped." Al chuckled.

"Sit Down Hun. I need to talk to you," Lorraine said. She wasn't sure what to expect from Al once she told him.

"Well this sounds serious," Al mused with a puzzled look on his face.

Lorraine decided just to blurt it out. "I'm planning on holding another séance." Before Al could respond she kept on talking. "I know it wasn't easy living with me these past few months, I missed a lot. The holidays, spending time with you, and I wasn't there for the girls."

"Then why do you want to go through that again? How can you think about doing that to us again?" Al questioned.

" I have to know if I was actually communicating with my Uncle Ed that night. I need to know what happen to him and those men. It's important to me." She looked at him with pleading eyes.

"First of all you don't know if you can contact the same exact spirit. If you can't, I'm afraid that you'll shut down like you did this last time. You were so angry, not to mention depressed. No one could talk to you. No one wanted too." Al started to raise his voice.

"I won't let that happened. I've learned a lot from that experience. I promise."

"You don't know that. You think you can control yourself and everything around you, but you can't." Al stood firm, even though he knew he would eventually give in.

After a hour of going back and forth Lorraine got her way. She vowed to Al it would be different this time. Little did she know just how different and dangerous it was going to be.

Now that Lorraine had Al's reluctant approval she could let everyone in the group know that she was planning on having another séance. She first called her brother Jim, then her Aunt Marie.

"Are you sure this is what you want to do?" Jim asked before he would agree to being involved. "You were pretty messed up over that bull shit Mitch put you through."

"I can always count on you to say what's on your mind ," Lorraine quipped. "But, to answer your question, yes this is what I want to do. Please, I need you to be there for me."

There was a long silence, and then a sigh. "Alright, I'll be there," Jim relented.

Lorraine had gotten everyone to agree to participate in the séance. She needed all the same people, in hopes that she could recreate the same energy as before. Now her and Chris needed to decide on a date. They had no new information to ensure they could contact the same spirit. All they had was her Uncle Ed's photo. Then Chris suggested that they hold it on the evening of his birthday which was coming up on February Fifth. Lorraine agreed, that would be perfect. That date was something personal to him.

It was a few nights before the séance when Kat asked, " are you sure want to put yourself through this again Mom? The last time you did this you were just miserable afterwards."

"I know, and I can't say I'm sorry enough for the way I acted. I just have to try one more time. I need to know if that was really was my uncle."

Well I'm just glad I won't be home that night. Smoke and I are going to the movies," Kat snorted sarcastically.

"Maybe Leann and Maggie can tag along with you," Lorraine hinted.

"You don't have to worry. They're going to have a sleep over at Deb's house across the street." Kat stated, as she rolled her eyes.

"Hey look Katelyn," Lorraine's tone changed to anger."It wasn't but a few months ago you and Maggie were close. Just because you have a boyfriend doesn't make you a grown up. Boys come and go, but family and close friends are forever."

"Yah, a few months ago you were so wrapped up in yourself, you forgot about your family. Now your gonna do it again."

"*Katelyn*" *That is uncalled for,*" Lorraine shouted.

"*Yah well, it's the truth,*" Kat shouted back and walked away.

The sad thing was, Lorraine knew that Katelyn was right. She did ignore her family. She lost sight of what was really important. Now she feared that she would do it again.

Lorraine started to feel that same anger build up inside of her. Before it completely took over, she stood up and said aloud, "I am stronger this time, I won't let this come between me and my family again."

February 5th. 11pm

The night air was thick with humidity. The temperature outside was 38 degrees. The ground was damp and slushy. It wasn't the most ideal night to be out, but everyone showed up.

When the group started holding séances they were eager and excited. There was a mystery about the unknown. The possibility of speaking with someone who was long since gone from this earth. Now it just seemed forced. Something they had to do. More or less, something that Lorraine was obsessed with.

The table was set. The candles were in place. Ed's picture was in the middle of the table next to the glass of water. Once again the tape recorder was on the counter ready to record anything they may not be able to hear.

Everyone took their seats. The candles were lit and the lights were turned off. They held hands, closed their eyes , and said the prayer of protection before they started.

Lorraine began to breathe deeply as she went into a trance. Summoning Ed, she called out to the men on the ill fated submarine. A half an hour went by with no sign of movement in the glass of water. In fact there was nothing at all. Lorraine could feel the tension in the room growing. The group wanted to stop, they knew it was hopeless. Lorraine wouldn't let go. Her voice was getting louder, as she started to get angry.

"Ed I beseech you, make yourself known. Anyone from below come forth, now."

Just then she could feel her brother Jim's hand try to pull away from hers. He knew that she had just opened the door for any unknown entity to come in. Lorraine would not let go of Jim's hand. She was not going to let the chain be broken.

The room started to get hot, the water started to bubble. A stench filled the room. It smelled like burning flesh.

Outside Kat was sitting in Smoke's car. They had been parked in the driveway making out. Their hands groping at each other in a wild frenzy. Out of the corner of Kat's eye she caught what looked like a haze around the kitchen window. There also appeared to be an array of colors, red, yellow, and orange illuminating from the window. The colors almost looked like flames, it was as if something was on fire. Kat pushed Smoke away, and asked, "are you seeing what I see?"

"What the hell are you talking about?" Smoke moaned as he still tried to grope at her.

"Look....look at the fucking window, "Kat growled as she punched him in the chest.

"What the hell, you crazy bitch."

"Look," Kat screamed.

"What the hell is that? Is your house on fire?"

Kat pushed against the car door almost falling out. She slipped in the slushy snow while running across the street to get her sister Leann and Maggie. Frantically pounding on the door yelling for the both of them, the door jerked open. Before Leann could ask, Kat blurted out, "Something is wrong."

"What do you mean?" Leann questioned. Kat grabbed Leann's arm and pulled her out the door as Maggie followed.

"Look... look at the kitchen window," Kat said as she pointed. "That smell, that wasn't there a minute ago."

"Oh my God, that smells putrid. It smells like burning flesh," Maggie gagged, she was trying not to vomit.

"Leann go get Al, he's down the street at the bar," Kat ordered.

Leann ran down the street and into the bar. Al was sitting at the back table watching TV. He saw Leann come through the door. Getting up, he grabbed his coat. She didn't need to say anything. He could tell by the look on her face that something was terribly wrong.

Pulling at Maggie's shirt Kat said, "come on we can't wait for Al. Something is wrong." They could hear what sounded like furniture being upended.

They both went running in, the stench and heat were unbearable. They made their way to the kitchen and saw that Jim had Lorraine pinned against the wall choking her.

Chris screamed at Kat, "do something, he's too strong. I can't stop him."

Kat did the only thing that she could think of. Grabbing the frying pan off of the stove, she hit her Uncle Jim as hard as she could in the back of the head. He dropped to his knees, then onto the floor and didn't move. Chris stepped over him and ran to Lorraine's side grapping her. She took her to the nearest chair, sitting her down before she passed out.

Al burst in yelling, "what the hell is going on and what the fuck is that smell?" He ran to Lorraine's side to see if she was alright.

"I think I just killed Uncle Jim." Kat was shaking. Her voice was trembling.

Once again Al demanded to know, "what the hell happened here?"

"Jim tried to choke Lorraine," Chris managed to eke out. Her voice breaking up. She had never seem Al so angry.

"All right.... Katelyn, Leann, and Maggie, I want you girls to go back across the street and stay there. Oh and Katelyn, send your boyfriend home now. Chris I need you to help me check Jim and get him up into a chair."

They were able to find a pulse and get him seated. Chris ran and got a rag and soaked in cold water to put on the back of his neck. Al opened the window to let some cool air in and hoped he could rid the house of that horrible smell. Eventually Jim started to come to too. He had a massive headache and a bump to match. As far as Al could see, everyone seemed to be okay. Which was good because he was through will all it. He'd had enough.

"I'm through with all the bullshit. I don't know what went on here tonight and I don't really care. I'm done with all this séance shit." He looked at Lorraine, "your brother could have killed you. I knew this wasn't a good idea and I should have said no. I'm putting my foot down. *No More!* I want everyone to leave, *Now!*" No one argued. They knew better.

Lorraine looked at Al and got up. "Please whatever you're going to say to me can it wait until tomorrow. I just want to go to bed."

"I have nothing else to say. I'm done. If you want to keep having these séances, I'm leaving, for good."

Most of the night Lorraine tossed and turned. She needed to

know if there was anything on the tape. She needed to know why her brother would try and kill her, but she decided it would be best to wait until Al left for work. Lorraine couldn't help but think, that whole night felt wrong. No one was in the right frame of mind, including herself. She needed to know what evil spirit she may have invited into their home. As Al was leaving he didn't say a word to Lorraine when he walked out the door. The silence was louder than anything he could have said.

Pouring herself a cup of coffee, Lorraine sat down at the kitchen table with the tape recorder in front of her. She almost afraid to press the play button, Lorraine's hand shook when she finally did.

As it played she could hear what sounded like faint screams. It sounded like the screams of people in agony. Some of the voices were moaning even begging for the pain to stop. She could hear what sounded like whips cracking, as the voices screamed for the torture to end. While there were other voices that laughed with delight, enjoying the pain that they were inflicting.

The temperature in the room started to rise. A slight stench started to fill the room. It was the same odor from the night before.

Through the screams came a voice that called to her. It was a low pitched gravelly voice that hissed like a snake. "Lorraine do you know who I am? I have many names, but you know me as the devil." More agonizing screams were heard in the background. There was a hideous sizzling sound. The sound of an iron branding flesh. An overwhelming stench filled the room that made Lorraine instantly nauseous.

"Come and join me Lorraine," the voice hissed. "You can talk to as many spirits as you like. They can tell what it's like to be down here. Of course, none of them thought that their small indiscretions in life would have condemned their souls eternally to Hell, but then no one ever does," the voice taunted her with laughter.

Becoming more terrified. Lorraine slammed her hand down on the buttons shutting the tape recorded off. Sitting there trembling,

Lorraine didn't know what to do or where to turn. She knew that she couldn't tell Al. Everyone else was ordered to leave the night before. Lorraine wasn't sure if they would want to speak to her again. She had to talk to someone. The fear was consuming her with every passing minute.

Chris's phone rang. She snatched it up on the first ring. "I need to see you, please," Lorraine begged.

"Oh thank God you're okay," Chris sighed with relief.

"Meet me at the restaurant." Lorraine whispered into the phone, afraid someone may be listening.

Sitting in the back booth of the restaurant, the color had completely drained from Chris's face as she listened to the tape. "Chris I am so scared," tears filled Lorraine's eyes. "I thought that I was so smart, so strong. I thought that I knew how to control a séance. Look what I've done, I invited the most evil of spirits into my home around my family and friends. What am I going to do? I can't tell Al. He's on the verge of leaving me."

"We're not going to do anything," Chris countered. "The best thing to do is stop before we make this any worse. Your gonna go home and take care of Al and the girls. Get your family back. We're not going to put anymore energy into this. So just put this behind you."

Chris was right and Lorraine knew it. If they were to try and put any more energy into this, it would take on a life of its own. It had already gotten out of control. Taking Chris's advise, Lorraine went home and made dinner hoping that it would be the start of a new beginning. She did want to put this behind her and get back to the way things were between her and Al and the girls.

Sadly they ate dinner in silence. As much as Lorraine tried to make conversation, no one wanted to talk. The girls hurried through dinner, excusing themselves by saying, "we have to go, we're going to be late."

Al did the same, "I'm going down the street to the tavern for a beer."

Lorraine cried as she put the dinner away and washed the last of the dishes. With no one home, Lorraine decided that there was no point in staying up. Tired, emotionally and physically she turned in for the night.

When she awoke it was so hot and hazy that it didn't feel like she was in her bedroom anymore. The smell was horrible. All at once Lorraine felt something nipping at her ankles. Then something began scratching at her legs, followed by the sound of laughter. "I don't know who's in here, but if you don't leave I'm going to call the police," Lorraine threatened. Without warning there was a sharp pain that ripped across her back, causing her to scream in agony. Little creatures were clawing at the open flesh hanging from her back. The pain was excruciating.

Then came a voice that she recognized. "I told you to join me Lorraine," the voice hissed. "You refused. No one refuses me!"

Next there was the sizzle of a hot iron against her flesh. Letting out such a blood curdling scream, Lorraine jolted straight up. Covered in sweat, she realized that it was all a horrible nightmare. The bedroom looked the same as it did when she laid down. The dreams continued every night for over a week. Each one worse than the one before. As soon as Al left, Lorraine got on the phone, "Chris, I need you to meet me at the restaurant."

"Are you alright?" Chris questioned.

"Just meet me."

Chris was already in the back booth waiting for Lorraine to arrive. "Oh my God, are you okay? What happened?" Chris was afraid of what she might hear. Sitting there listening to every detail of Lorraine's dreams, Chris was horrified.

"I don't know what I'm going to do. I haven't slept in over a week." Lorraine was so exhausted, she couldn't even cry.

"I think I know what we can do. Can you get out of the house tonight and meet me in the city at St. Casmir's church? The doors are usually unlocked this time of year so the homeless have someplace to sleep if they need one. Just make sure you bring the tape," Chris said firmly.

Nodding in agreement, Lorraine left. On the way home she thought how no one would even notice that she had gone back out. Al stayed out late, and when he did come home he would sleep on the couch. Regardless she needed to clear her mind. Whatever Chris had planned for the both of them to do, Lorraine needed to concentrate.

When she arrived at the church it was 11:45pm. Chris was already waiting outside for her. "I checked inside and the church is empty. We need to do this fast, before somebody shows up," Chris insisted.

"Do what? You haven't told me what it is we're going to do, and what is that in your hand?" Lorraine questioned.

"Come on, we need to go to the altar." Once they were in front of the altar Chris set a small pan on the floor. "You remembered to bring the tape didn't you?"

"I have it right here," Lorraine looked puzzled.

"Good put the tape in the pan. I got some holy water from the vestibule. We're gonna set the tape on fire and then put holy water on the ashes."

Before putting it in the pan, Lorraine pulled out some of the tape in hopes that it would burn faster. Chris set the tape on fire with a lighter that she had brought with. It burned slowly at first. Then all at once the tape was engulfed in flames. A black cloud of thick smoke rose from the pan. It took the shape of something indescribably eerie. Chris decided that this would be a good time to pour the holy water into the pan. When she poured the water on the flames, the smoke appeared to be sucked back into the pan as the fire went out. All that was left were ashes.

"Do you think that it's over?" Lorraine asked.

"I hope so." Chris grabbed Lorraine and hugged her as tight as she could. "I think we should sprinkle the ashes by the statue of our Lord, that will help protect you. I also want you to stay at my house tonight, it's late and you need to get some sleep," Chris urged.

Lorraine couldn't remember the last time she had a good night's sleep. Laying there she realized that it was over.

It took some time, but Lorraine and Al rekindled their relationship. They never spoke about the events that happened on the night she held the last séance. Al would never know about the nightmares and she would never tell him about the tape.

Leann was in high school now and she was a straight A student, which made Lorraine proud.

Even though Maggie wasn't Lorraine's biological daughter she felt honored that Maggie was comfortable enough to call her mom. She knew that after the loss of her mother, Maggie didn't have an easy life.

Katelyn was pregnant with twins. Lorraine busied herself by getting things ready for their arrival. She decided that it was best to concentrate on the living.

Part 5

Footsteps in the Night

Chapter 16

Things seemed to have come full circle for Maggie Stanczyk Jacobs. She grew up and went out into the world, got married and had kids of her own. After her divorce in 1984, Maggie had no choice but to move back home. Trying to raise two boys without a job wasn't the life she wanted for them to grow up in. She wanted them to have all the things that they needed.

She had always loved the town that she grew up in. It was a peaceful place tucked inside a world of chaos. Maggie was born in a Polish neighborhood on the south side of Chicago. Her father worked as a machinist for a company off of 22nd and Western Ave. He was later transferred to the company's second plant forty miles west of the city. They moved to Westmont, which was the same town where Maggie's grandmother lived.

Westmont was founded in 1872 and didn't begin to flourish until 1917. The neighborhood had a collection of older frame homes that were built in the early 1920's. The houses were still well maintained, with posies that lined the walkways that led up to the front door. It gave you the feeling of an old world country charm that made you want to come in and stay for awhile. The street that they lived on was lined with elm trees. In their back yard grew a cherry, apple, and pear tree.

When you drove through town it made you feel as if you were

back in the twenties. There were baskets of morning glories that hung from the street lights with a Ben Franklin's Five and Dime, and an old time grocery store with the original hard wood floors. Maggie loved to shop there sometimes. All the stores in town looked like they were from an era long since gone.

Things between Maggie and her father had gotten better. He was sick. He'd had a series of small strokes. Maggie thought that it wasn't really a blessing to see someone that you love sick, but it did force him to stop drinking. She felt that if he hadn't the alternative would have been worse. The abusive episodes that followed his drinking, had also stopped.

He was thrilled to be a grandfather and he loved his grandkids. He nick named one button nose and the other Jessie James.

"How come you call Creed, Jessie James?" Maggie asked.

"Because I don't think the name Creed goes with James," her father replied.

"Do you know one of the things that I remember from when I was a teenager is, that when my friends called and asked for me by the name Maggie, you would always say, you mean Magdalene?"

"I know, it's how I was raised. It was a sign of respect, you always called a person by their given name," her father said. He also went on to say, "there was a lot of things that I did back then, and some of those things that I did were wrong, very wrong, and I am so sorry."

"It's okay, it's over and done with now," Maggie assured him.

"I'm just glad you felt that you could come home," her father said.

Maggie had no idea that her home coming would be short lived. Things would take a turn. It was early afternoon when her father walked out of his room and collapsed in the kitchen. Maggie called an ambulance, Creed was still in his highchair eating lunch at the time his grandfather had gotten sick. He kept saying, "bye grandpa" as the EMT's were getting ready to take him to the hospital. Maggie didn't realize how final that goodbye really was. The day her father was supposed to come home from the hospital was the day he died. Just like when her mother died, Maggie knew before she was told, that her father was gone.

Thinking back, Maggie remembered when her Uncle Ray died. He was at work and had been missing for almost two hours. They later found him in the men's bathroom dead, he had suffered a massive heart attack. Maggie's grandmother told her that while she was taking her afternoon nap in her easy chair, she was awaken by someone holding her hand. When her grandmother opened her eyes to see who it was, there was no one there. She remembered looking at the clock and it was 2:36pm, the doctors had estimated that was around the time that her son passed away. Maggie had thought, "maybe it was possible for the people that we love to visit us one last time before they leave this world forever."

Maggie had thought that no matter how old you are when you lose your parents you still feel like an orphan. Maggie's father left her the house, so she was at least able to put a roof over her boy's heads. Now all she needed to do was find a job. Kat's younger sister Leann whom preferred to be called Lee now, moved in with her. She was like a sister to Maggie.

Jack, who was Maggie's cousin let her know, "the company that I work for is hiring. The only problem is, the job is on second shift." After thinking about it Maggie accepted the job. Andrew Corporation was a good company to work for and she needed the money to support her sons. Everything seemed to be falling into place. She just needed to find someone to babysit, someone that she would be able to trust. Her kids were young. Luke was three and Creed was a year and a half. They were her world.

Chapter 17

Maggie had started to adjust, the realization that her father was gone started to sink in. She was also getting adjusted to her new job and the hours on second sift. Maggie would get home after midnight, relax for awhile and go to bed. Lee also worked second shift so it was nice to have someone to talk to about how the day went.

Maggie had found a babysitter that was willing to work those hours. Theresa was forty years old and single. She rented a room in the boarding house behind the flower shop in town. She thought that babysitting would be a great way to make some extra money, but after awhile Maggie became dissatisfied with her. Theresa would always leave the house a mess while putting the boys to bed way too early. It was almost as if she didn't want to be bothered with them, but yet, she felt that she deserved a raise.

Maggie did get concerned when Theresa claimed she was hearing noises. She had even called the police on several occasions. She said that one night she had heard a banging sound on the right side of the house. Then another night she said that she had heard footsteps on the front porch, followed by a light tapping on the window. There also was the night Theresa claimed she heard such a loud bang against the windows that they shook, she was actually surprised that the windows didn't break. The police were never able to find anything. They actually were starting to look at Theresa as someone that was wasting their time.

Maggie started to worry when her three year old son Luke would just sit on his bed and point to the corner of his room and say, "play, can I play with her?" I want to play with her Mommy." Maggie thought that the way Theresa was acting when it came to the noises she claimed to be hearing, was starting to cause the boys to image strange things.

Maggie finally made the decision to let Theresa go. She didn't have a backup plan and she needed her job, but the way Theresa was acting was getting out of hand, she was starting to scare the boys. Maggie didn't want them to think that there was a boogie man behind every door. She had grown up with a lot of fear instilled in her from her mother. Maggie wanted her boys to be strong.

It turned out that Lee's mother, Lorraine needed a job. She had run into some financial hardships since Al passed away five years ago, and could really use the money. She took the train in from the city and would stay at the house Monday through Friday.

Lorraine was what some people would call eccentric, she was fascinated with the spirit world, séances, and paranormal studies. Lorraine was up front, honest, and a strong women. Maggie had never felt comfortable calling anyone else mom. She felt that it would be a betrayal to her real mother, but it felt right to call Lorraine mom. She loved kids, so Maggie knew the boys were in good hands.

Chapter 18

It was June eighth and the day of Luke's birthday party at Show Biz Pizza. He was turning five and it seemed like time was really starting to slip away. There were some last minute errands Maggie needed to run. She had to go to K-mart and get name tags and extra decorations. As usual Creed wanted to go and Maggie said no. His only interest was in what toy he might be able to try and con her into buying him.

The car was parked in the back by the garage. Maggie noticed that both the windows were rolled down. She thought it was strange since she hadn't used the car yet. Just then, Maggie found herself distracted when she looked up to see someone looking down at her from the second story window. That was where her father always sat when he built his model cars. He sometimes just enjoyed looking out the window watching the day go by.

Maggie shook it off and got in the car. She had gotten two blocks down and stopped at the stop sign, when all of a sudden she heard a voice. Then someone jumped up from between the car seats. The voice said, "are we there yet?" It was her son Creed he had laid in wait curled up on the floor in the back of the car. He was determined to go to the store with her one way or the other. Since it was hot outside he had the sense to roll the windows down while he was waiting. He just didn't have the sense to stay down long enough until they got to the store. Maggie promptly took him back home. Lee was getting ready for work so Maggie went into her room and asked, "by any chance did you go up stairs for anything?"

"No why?"

"I was getting into the car when I looked up and I thought that I saw someone staring down at me from the upstairs window."

"That was probably just your dad," Lee replied.

Maggie didn't rule it out, she had always felt that there were some things that you just couldn't explain. Since her father had bled to death, some people say that you simply just get tired and drift out of consciousness. Could it be possible that he just didn't know that he had passed away.

Since his death nearly two years ago there had been several odd occurrences.Thinking back, Maggie remembered walking past his room, her father appeared to be sitting on the bed just looking out into the hallway. She also remembered one afternoon in particular, while she was washing the dishes Maggie felt a rush of cold air across her back. It seemed as if someone had walked past her, but when she turned to look, no one was there.

The strangest incidence happened while Maggie was getting ready for work. In the mirror she saw the reflection of a shorter darker figure. It was too small to be her father. All these things reminded Maggie of her childhood. The strange voices, the shadows in her room that would disappear. Just then a chill ran through her as she whispered, "what if it's not my father."

Chapter 19

While walking up town, Maggie was surprised to see that Mr. Remic was still alive. He was on his hands and knees clipping away at his lawn. He was also wearing what appeared to be the same clothes that he wore anytime Maggie would see him when she was child. His clothes always looked tattered. He wore a ratty looking red and black long sleeve shirt no matter what the weather was like outside. He also wore dark work pants and a old tattered fedora. The skin on his face was so wrinkled from years of working out in the sun, that it was the texture of a sundried raisin. Maggie was more frightened by him now then she was when she younger.

This time he didn't speak to her like he did when Maggie was young. He seemed to just sense that she was walking by and slightly turned his head to stare as she passed. It didn't seem to matter that the seasons were changing and it was getting colder outside, he was just always out there.

Maggie remembered that when she was growing up the Remic's weren't a very friendly family. At least he wasn't. When the neighborhood kids would play outside he would just stare at them while doing his yard work. He especially paid quite a bit of attention to the girls, which now, Maggie realized that there was something very wrong with the way he would look at them.

Maggie also remembered when she was a little girl her mother let her sell girl scout cookies, but she would only let her go to the houses on their block. When she went to the Remic's house he answered the door. Mr. Remic was the only one home and what frightened most of the children in the neighborhood was he always looked so angry, so mean. So it was no surprise that when he answered the door Maggie just stood there and stared at him.

"Well, what do you want? What are ya staring at girl?" Mr. Remic shouted.

"I'm.....I'm selling girl scout cookies. Would you like to buy some?" Maggie managed to croak out, as she started to tremble.

He just stood there and eyed her up and down, and said, "maybe you should come in so I can see what you got."

Just then Mrs. Remic came walking around the corner. She had been at the market. When she saw Maggie she yelled, "what are ya doin here? You get on home."

By that time Maggie was half way down the stairs, she ran home and told her mother what happened. "I don't want to the sell cookies anymore," Maggie said as she sobbed.

Just as her mother was about to confront Mrs. Remic she was already at their front door. She had apologized for yelling and said that her husband was a diabetic and had no will power when it came to sweets. Now that Maggie was older she thought maybe he didn't have any will power when it came to little girls. She felt bad about thinking that, he could have been a very nice person, but she also thought that every neighborhood does have at least one strange neighbor. Then one day Maggie realized that she hadn't seen him for awhile and when she was talking to her neighbor Linda she had mentioned it.

"You must not have heard." Linda didn't know if it was a family member or a friend of the family but, she continued on and said, "they hadn't heard from Mrs. Remic for awhile so the police did a wellness check. When they went into the house the police found

Mrs. Remic on the kitchen floor, she had suffered a stroke and Mr. Remic had left her laying there for almost a week, while he kept tending to his lawn. They were both taken away and no one has heard anymore about them since."

"How horrible. Not being able to move or speak. Just being left on the floor to die," Maggie thought out loud.

Chapter 20

It was getting closer to Maggie's favorite holiday, Halloween. There was something magical about the month of October, all the fall colors were in bloom. The decorations were always proudly displayed at the beginning of the month. The skeletons were hung up and the headstones were put out on the front lawn. In keeping with the spirit of the holiday they would watch horror movies as often as they could. Both Maggie and Lee had always loved horror films. The more frighten that they were, made them even better.

One night while Maggie was at work Lee's mother said, "you have to call Maggie at work."

"Why, what's wrong?" Lee replied

"The lamp that Maggie has hanging in her room keeps turning on and off. I don't want her to be scared."

"Why would she be afraid of a lamp?"

"Because I think that someone is trying to communicate with me through the lamp. I think it may be some type of Morse code."

Reluctantly dialing the phone Lee was able to get through to Maggie. Holding back the laughter Maggie told her, "Lee, tell your mom that the lamp has a bad switch and if it's not turned off correctly and it gets bumped, it will flicker on and off."

It so happened that the lamp was very close to the head board of the bed. Lorraine had let the boys sleep in Maggie's room that night so every time they would roll over the head board would bump the lamp.

Maggie could hear Lee say to her mother, "the lamp has a bad switch Mom, that's all it is. There was no reason for me to call her."

Maggie couldn't resist, "Lee ask your mom if my toaster is sending her any messages."

Her mother insisted, "you can make fun of me all you want, but I know this means something and I'm writing it down."

Lorraine had to take care of some business in the city the next day with Chris, she was Lorraine's best friend of more than twenty five years. Lorraine had an appointment with Chris's lawyer. Her house had gone into foreclosure and Lorraine was desperate to do whatever she could to save it. The house had belonged to Al, and that was all she had left of him and the memories that they had shared together. She couldn't bear the thought of losing it. Once she had arrived at Chris's house Lorraine pulled out the paper that she had written down how often the lamp had blinked. Eagerly trying to figure out what it could possibly mean, Lorraine realized that they were now running late for her appointment. They both got in Chris's car and took off. When they had gotten to the intersection they had to take a detour because of a fatal car accident. A semi truck had gone through a red light and hit two vehicles that were turning left. At that point they both realized that if they would have left five minutes earlier, they would have been right in the middle of it. Lorraine looked at Chris and said, "do you realize how lucky we are, that could have been us."

When Lorraine finally returned to Maggie's, she informed both of them that the lamp was trying to warn her and Chris, they were both lucky enough to avoid that fatal car crash only by minutes. Lee's mom went on to say, "I know how these things work because I've studied to be a medium and was taught how to read the signs and signals."

Once again Maggie couldn't resist making a comment. "Well, I'm an extra large myself."

Which at that point Lee promptly kicked her under the table and muttered under her breath, "don't encourage her."

It was in Maggie's nature to make jokes, but she fully respected Loraine and what she believed in.

Chapter 21

Halloween was finally here and it always made Maggie feel like a kid at heart. It took her back to when she was young and her mother was still alive. They always had so much fun together. On Halloween every kid lived by a code. It was the candy code. It was every kids job, a sworn duty to pass along to every fellow trick or treater which houses gave out the best candy. Back then it was root beer barrels, pop rocks and candy cigarettes as far as the eye could see. Every kid was in their glory.

Maggie always took that day off from work. There was always so much to do. Luke was in kindergarten and they were going to have costume parade so the kids could show off their costumes. That year Luke was a pirate with a hook for a hand, an eye patch, and a parrot on his shoulder. Creed's costume was handmade. He was going to be a big green frog.

"Mom, how come I have to be the frog and Luke gets to be the pirate?" He complained.

"Well because, you can't sit still, you're always hopping around," Maggie laughed.

"That's okay, it's still a pretty cool costume," Creed said.

When Maggie took the boys out trick or treating she even wore a costume. That year she was a clown. She would often wear that same costume and entertain her friends kids when they were having their birthday parties. As usual the boys thought that they had struck the mother lode. After Maggie checked through all the candy she would decide what they could have and when.

"Awe mom, can we have some more candy? It is ours. Quit being so mean," Luke said as he pouted.

"Yah, that's not fair," Creed chimed in.

"Well this meanie says your done, now go play," Maggie said laughing.

The trick or treating started to taper off a little after five o'clock. There were always the older kids that would stretch it out to six or seven. That's usually when the pranks would begin.

At 8:30 Maggie and Lee had settled in to watch another horror movie. They heard a slight knocking on the screen door followed by a giggle. They both looked at each and thought that it was a little too late for any kids to be out, but Maggie grabbed the candy bowl and went to the door to find out no one was there. They both assumed it was a prank. They had started to watch the movie again when there was another knock followed by a giggle. Once again no one was there. It happened two more times when they heard something that sounded like pebbles being thrown onto the porch. Maggie went to check when she almost slipped on what appeared to be marbles. The sound they made reminded her of the noise she would hear as a young child when she would lay in bed at night, the sound of marbles hitting the floor. Maggie was a little unnerved and asked Lee, "do you think we should ask your mom what she thinks? She seems to be good at figuring out what things like this mean."

Lee just looked at her shaking her head, "have you completely lost your mind? It was probably someone pulling a prank on us." Maggie decided to leave it at that.

Things started to escalate and get stranger after that. The next night they were sitting in the kitchen drinking coffee catching up on how each other's week went. It was after midnight when they heard a noise in the basement that sounded like something fell. The dog even perked up when he heard the sound, but other than that he acted like he couldn't be bothered. Then it sounded like something else fell. Maggie got up and walked over to the door at the end of the hall. Opening it a crack, she looked towards the downstairs back door to make sure that it was still locked. She checked in on the boys to make sure they were still asleep and okay.

"What do you think we should do?" Maggie asked Lee. She was the more rational of the two of them. Just then there was another noise. So they decided to send the dog downstairs.

Ten minutes had passed when all of a sudden they heard Rex yelp. They waited, but they didn't hear anything else. Maggie tried calling for him, but she couldn't get him to come upstairs. She locked the door and decided to wait a little while to see if Rex would come back up on his own. After fifteen minutes they heard him at the door. When Maggie let him in, he appeared to physically look okay, but he had shot past her and cowered in the corner. Neither one of them knew what to think. They didn't dare call the police. Theresa had called them so much that they were afraid the police wouldn't come when they really needed them.

They stayed up for another hour just in case there was anything else that might happen, but as time pasted everything seemed to be okay. They decided to call it a night and went to bed.

Chapter 22

It was coming up on November third, Maggie's twenty sixth birthday. It just so happened that it fell on a Saturday. What Maggie didn't know was that her friends had been making plans since the beginning of October to throw her a surprise party. Lee and Kat knew that see had never had one.

Lee had contacted Maggie's cousin Jack to find out which of their co-workers she should invite to the party. Jack could also pass along the invitations. They already had it set up with Linda who lived across the street to watch the boys. Linda told Maggie that the boys were invited for a sleep over with Danny. The boys were thrilled and Maggie thought out loud, "I can have a night out."

Jack told Lee, "I let about fifteen people know about the party. I know at least eleven can make it. The others may have to work if they get the material in for a rush job."

"I think that's a good number, with Kat, you, and your brother, plus myself that will be perfect. Now all's I have to do is get Maggie out of the house for awhile."

"Why don't you tell Maggie that you want her to go shopping with you," Kat said.

"You know Maggie hates to shop," Lee reminded her.

"What women isn't born with the shopping gene?" Kat asked.

"Maggie, that's who."

They finally decided that Lee was going to ask Maggie to go with her to drop off something at a friend's. Laura, who was a friend and co-worker of Lee's needed to borrow a dress for a wedding. "I can tell her that I'm not really sure how to get there," Lee said.

Kat agreed, "That would be perfect. Everyone knows you have no directional skills."

"Hah funny, not," Lee snorted.

Saturday was finally here and Maggie took the bait. She knew just how bad Lee's scene of direction was. They left at 4pm. Lee needed to keep Maggie out of the house for at least two hours.

They finally made it to Laura's house at 4:30. "I just made a fresh pot of coffee, come on in and have a cup," Laura offered. She knew that Lee had to keep Maggie occupied for a while.

They finally pulled into the back yard around 6:45. "Hey, since the boys are at a sleep over, why don't we go to the movies?" Maggie suggested.

"Well why don't we see what's playing. I got the news paper this morning," Lee said.

They headed up the back stairs, Lee making sure that Maggie went first. The minute she opened the door Maggie was blasted with, "SURPRISE". Startled, she almost knocked Lee down the stairs.

"Holy shit," Maggie exclaimed panting.

"You really didn't have a clue, did you?" Lee and Kat said laughing.

"No....no I did not," Maggie said. "Thank-you....all of you." Maggie was truly surprised to see that some of the people that she worked with had shown up. She thought to herself how lucky she was to have the friends that she did.

Kat ordered pizza. There was beer for those that drank, and music. They talked and laughed for a good part of the evening.

Then Gary, one of Maggie's friends from work noticed she had an Uno card game. "Hey, let's play Uno. I haven't played this in forever, man," he yelled out.

" Yah, let's play strip Uno," Allan added.

"Shut up, sit down, and keep your clothes on that drunk ass of yours," Gary told him.

Awwwwwe man," Allen slurred.

Maggie laughed and said, "keep it up and your cut off. No more beer for you."

By that time everyone was having a blast. They agreed, "sure, why not, we'll play."

The card game went on for almost two hours when Allen got up and said, "I'm gonna go out back and have a smoke and get some air."

"Just don't get lost or pass out in someone else's yard. We don't want to have to send out a search party to look for ya." Jack warned him.

"Yah, Yah, Yah," Alan muttered.

"We're never gonna see him again. He'll get lost somewhere," Lee said laughing .

Everyone talked and joked around for another hour when Lee said, "hey maybe Allan really did get lost."

"Oh shit I didn't realize he's been gone that long," Kat said.

"I'll go look for him," Gary said.

"No, you sit and relax. I'll go," Lee offered.

Lee went out back to find him just sitting in a chair staring up at the night sky. "Are you okay?" She asked.

"Yah, I'm fine, it's just so nice out here tonight. The breeze feels so good," Allan replied.

What happened next took Lee by surprise. Allan got up, grabbed her, and kissed her. Lee thought he was good looking, but the problem was, Allan also thought he was good looking. She didn't want to be just another one of his conquests. Allan was a nice guy, but he made it clear that he wasn't looking for anything serious. Lee was still a virgin, and she was proud of that. Things started to heat up,

Allan kept groping her. Starting to feel uncomfortable, Lee finally pushed him away.

"Stop," Lee said firmly.

"Hey I thought that you were getting into it as much as I was?"

"Look, I like you and I think that your cute, but I don't want to have sex with you."

"You don't?" Allan said, with a stunned look on his face.

"No I don't."

"Look, I'm sorry. I guess I had a little too much to drink," Allan said apologetically.

"It's okay, just pull yourself together and come in when you're ready. Everybody's wondering what happened to ya," Lee said.

"I'll be in, give me a few minutes."

Lee turned and walked back into the house.

"Well, where the hell is he?" Gary asked

"He was just sittin outside. He's coming in," Lee answered.

Allan was starting to sober up. He felt bad that he had tried to take advantage of Lee. When he tried the back door it wouldn't open. He had thought that Lee may have locked it, although the doorknob was turning. He didn't want to start banging on it so, he just kept pushing against it. All of a sudden it felt like someone jerked the door open. When he walked in there was nobody there. He noticed that it was ice cold. There seemed to be a haze coming up from the basement. He walked over to see what it was when he felt like something was pulling him in. Something or someone that seemed angry. Just then the upstairs back door opened and broke the trance that he was in. It was Gary, "hey, where the hell have you been? It's getting late man. I think it's time to go. We got a forty five minute drive."

"Yah, yah that's cool. Let's go," Alan said, as he kept looking over his shoulder.

It was about two in the morning by the time everyone left.

Maggie couldn't believe that all those people had showed up for her. "I had the best time," Maggie said. "Thank-you both for doing this for me."

"We're glad that you had a good time, and that everything turned out great. You deserve it." Kat and Lee both said, giving her a hug.

Chapter 23

Thanksgiving was a few weeks away. "What do you think about the both of us cooking Thanksgiving dinner and inviting some people over?" Lee suggested.

"Well, I've never cooked a turkey before, have you?" Maggie asked.

"No, but how hard could it be? I just thought that since your birthday party went so well, we should entertain more. Maybe we should invite people over for dinner once and a while," Lee said.

"I did enjoy my party," Maggie said, as she smiled thinking about it. "Okay, let's make a turkey. Who should we invite?"

"Well what about your Aunt Rose and your cousins Jack and Jason?" Lee said.

"Who else?" Maggie asked.

"I was thinking just them," Lee said.

"That's it?" Maggie asked.

"Yah," Lee said. Looking at Maggie with a sheepish expression on her face.

"Alright what gives?" Maggie wanted to know.

"Alright, I kinda like your cousin," Lee admitted.

"Well it can't be Jack, he's gay........so, you got the hots for Jason?" Maggie teased.

"Ha ha, but if you must know, yes I like Jason. I have for a long time," Lee confessed.

"I thought that Allan kinda liked you?" Maggie asked.

"Yah well, when I went outside to look for him, we started to kiss. Then he started to grab me and, I just didn't know if I liked him that way. I just met him that day," Lee told her.

He didn't force himself on you did he?" Maggie demanded.

"No, no, he stopped when I told him too. He also apologized," Lee stated firmly.

"You're sure?" Maggie questioned.

"Yes I'm sure," Lee assured her.

"Okay, well let's do this dinner thing then," Maggie said.

They went shopping and got everything that they needed for dinner. Maggie had gotten her Aunt Rose's recipe for kolackys. Her aunt's were always the best. Maggie made them the night before along with a cheese cake.

They bought a twelve pound turkey and planned on making homemade stuffing. "Alright, I think we can do this," Maggie said. They rubbed butter under the skin of the turkey. Added the seasonings and put it in the oven. The next thing to do was make the stuffing. Everything seemed to be going great for their first time cooking a turkey.

Maggie's Aunt and two cousins arrived at three o'clock. The smell of the holiday filled the air. Maggie and Lee were in the kitchen getting the turkey out the oven. While they were lifting the turkey out of the pan they heard a plop. "What the hell is that?" Maggie asked.

Lee looked at a little closer and said, "I think that something fell out from the front of the turkey. It looks like the neck bone with some other stuff in a plastic bag."

"I hope it didn't ruin the turkey being cooked in there like that," Maggie said.

When they went to look at the bag closer it was gone. "Where the hell it go?" Lee asked.

Just then they heard something behind them. As they turned to look they saw Rex in the corner enjoying his own Thanksgiving dinner. He was chewing on the bag that fell out of the turkey.

"Okay, this never happened," Maggie said.

"Agreed," Lee replied.

Even with the slight mishap earlier the dinner turned out delicious. They all sat at the kitchen table and reminisced about holidays from the past, drank coffee, and had desert.

Maggie had gone to the video store and rented the movie Money Pit starring Tom Hanks. She thought that would be a movie that everyone would enjoy. Lee had different plans for her and Jason. There was an old pool table in the back half of the basement with a couple of old couches and a stereo. It was okay for family. It wasn't anything fancy.

"Hey, why don't you and I go downstairs and shoot a game of pool? Your always sayin how good ya are." Lee said sarcastically.

Jason thought about it. "Okay your on."

They went downstairs, and Maggie put the movie in.

After awhile Jason put down his pool cue. He walked behind Lee as she was bent over trying to take her shot. He grabbed her around the waist and pulled her into him. She straighten up and he kissed the back of her neck. He ran his one hand up to her right breast and his left hand down between her legs. She let out a deep moan as he walked her over to the couch. He undid her jeans and pushed them down. Then turning her around he laid her down on the couch and thrust himself inside of her. Lee had never made love before. She felt like she was going to burst from all the different sensations that were going through her body. She just wanted to scream out, it felt so good. After they finished they held each other in silence.

"Are you okay?" Jason asked.

"Can I tell you something?" Lee asked.

"Sure, after what we just did you can tell me anything," Jason chuckled.

"I've never done that before," Lee told him.

"Wow, I guess I feel honored that you felt that strongly about me, to give me such a special gift." They held each other and kissed. They were lost in each other's embrace. Then, all of a sudden the silence was broken by the sound of footsteps.

Lee looked past Jason. "Did you hear that?"

"Hear what?"

"Ssssh......footsteps, I heard footsteps."

"I didn't hear anything," Jason assured her.

Just then Lee sat up. She thought that she had seen a glimpse of red hair.

"It might just be Maggie. Maybe she came down here to see what we were doing and got embarrassed, that's all. Are you sure you're alright? Your shivering," Jason said, cradling her in his arms.

"Maybe we should go up stairs its freezing down here," Lee said.

"Yah you're right, I didn't notice it before," Jason agreed.

Lee and Jason made their way back upstairs. The movie was over and Rose, Jack and Maggie were drinking coffee and eating some of the kolackys.

"Hey Maggie, did you need us for something when you went downstairs?" Jason asked.

"What are ya talking about? I didn't go downstairs for anything."

"Are you sure?" Lee asked as the color drained from her face.

"I think I'd know whether I went down there or not. Is everything okay?" Maggie asked.

"Yah everything is fine," Lee said.

Maggie's Aunt and cousins left at ten o'clock. She asked Lee, "what was that about? Asking if I went downstairs?"

"I heard footsteps and saw what I thought was a flash of red hair. I thought maybe it was you, and then you got embarrassed because Jason and I were, well ya know."

"Oh really." Maggie said, moving her eyebrows up and down.

"Yah, it was pretty terrific," Lee said with a smile.

"Well I'm happy for you."

Chapter 24

Maggie was happy to see that the boys seemed to be well adjusted. Their father never came to visit. He didn't even call, but surprisingly they never really asked about him either. They were typical boys saying, "Mom he took my toy, Mom he's looking at me, Mom he won't stop touching me." Maggie said to herself , "if I had a nickel for every time I heard mom he's doing something, I'd be a millionaire."

All though they had their moments Luke was Creed's big brother and protector. They were playing in the living room when Maggie took the opportunity to take some things out to the garage. While she was out back Creed started to cough and since Luke didn't know that she had just gone out to the garage for a few minutes he made Creed lay down on the couch while he called an ambulance. When Maggie came back in she had heard him talking to someone. When she went into the living room she could hear a voice on the phone asking, "is everything alright ?" Maggie grabbed the phone and realized Luke had called 911. The women on the other end seemed skeptical, but Maggie reassured her that everything was okay.

She realized that Luke would never do anything to hurt his brother. A couple of days later the boys were playing outside with their friend Danny and Bruce. They knew Creed was afraid to go in the basement. Bruce took Creed's toy and threw it downstairs and ran off. Creed slowly took one step at a time looking towards the open basement door. When he reached the bottom he stood in the doorway looking in. Creed could see his toy by the washing machine. He had a plan, he would run in and grab it and run out as fast as he could. Creed was just about to make his move when he felt someone push him in and slam the door. He started to scream and pound on the door for someone to let him out. The door just wouldn't open, it seemed to be locked.

Maggie was out in front raking up the last little bit of leaves when she heard Creed screaming. She ran to the back door and down the basement steps. The other kids followed to see what all the commotion was about. Maggie tried to get the door open but it seemed to be stuck. "Mom open the door, get me out of here, I'm scared," Creed wailed. She forced the door open and Creed ran past her, up the stairs and out the back door. She caught up to him and told him, "calm down. Everything is going to be okay." Creed just kept crying and telling her how scared he was. He said that there had to be someone else down there. He heard someone behind him laughing, but he couldn't see who it was because it was so dark down there.

Maggie started to scold Luke and the other boys. Luke said, "I didn't know that they were going to do that to him."

"We're sorry. We only threw is toy down there. We never pushed him," both Danny and Bruce told her.

By then Creed had started to calm down. He was more concerned about his toy now. "Mom can you please go down there and get it? It's my favorite transformer."

Maggie went downstairs and turned the lights on and looked around, but she couldn't find it. She asked him, "where do you think they may have thrown it?"

"It was by the washing machine." Creed told her.

"Sweetie, there's nothing there."

"But mom, I know it is, I saw it."

Maggie told him, "I'll go back down there and look again, but I'll have to do it later. It's getting late. I need to get dinner started."

"Mom it's my favorite dinobot . It's grimlock," Creed pleaded.

" I promise. I will go back downstairs and find it."

Maggie knew even as she made that promise she probably wouldn't find it. It would be like all the other toys that went missing down through the years, they just seemed to vanish.

Chapter 25

Christmas was a week away. It was going to take that long for Maggie to wrap all of the boys gifts that she had bought them. She had started to shop for their presents in September and hid them upstairs.

Lee teased her, "you bought way too much. You're going to spoil them."

There was a part of her that felt sad and alone. Her parents were gone and she knew that the boy's father wouldn't bother with them, let alone buy them any gifts. Maggie felt she needed to make up for that.

When Maggie was young her family had traditions. On Christmas Eve they would go to her grandmother's house to exchange gifts, but before they would leave the house Maggie and her brother Philip would leave a glass of milk and a plate of cookies out for Santa Claus. After the festivities at their grandmother's, they would go home and see if Santa had come. The milk would be gone and the cookies were eaten.

When Maggie was older she found out that it was her Uncle Ray that would slip out the back door while they were exchanging gifts, and then go to the house and put the Christmas presents under the tree so the kids would think that Santa had come. The one year Maggie remembered the most was that she had gotten the doll house that she had wanted and a pink dress with rabbit fur trim around the collar and sleeves.

Maggie was happy that the boys Aunts and Uncles still included them in their Christmas Eve activity. No matter what had happened between Maggie and their brother, they actually still treated her as a part of their family. Her and the kids were invited to spend the evening there, because Santa was planning to visit.

On that night she had decided to take her father's 1964 Ford Galaxy 500 that he had left her. Maggie's father loved to collect vintage cars. She could remember down through the years that he had a 1957 Chevy, a 1952 Hudson Wasp, and even an Edsel. Whenever she told people that, they would laugh and say an Edsel. She never quite understand why. His favorite wasn't the Galaxy though, it was a celery green colored 1954 Hudson Hornet. That was his pride and joy. It was once featured in a classic car magazine. The ford was always kept in the garage. It was a real beauty, all original with low miles. White with red leather interior. Her father had bought it off the show room floor in the late seventies.

When they went out that evening Maggie had left the overhead door to the garage open. It was cold and there was snow in the forecast. She didn't want to get out of the car and fight to get the door open when they got back home.

It was a little after eleven when she pulled into the alley. Maggie backed the car into the garage. Both the boys were asleep in the back seat still holding on to some of the toys that Santa had brought them. She went over to the light switch and flipped it on. The lights wouldn't go on, so she tried flipping the switch a couple of more times and still nothing. Maggie just assumed that a fuse had blown out. The fuse box was down in the basement and was old, so it wasn't unusual for a fuse to blow out every now and then.

She leaned into the car to get the kids out. All of a sudden she heard click, click, then the lights went on. She stood up and muttered under her breath, "what the hell." She looked franticly from the side door to the overhead door and didn't see anyone or anything. Not realizing her own strength she grabbed both of the boys and pulled them out from the back seat of the car. Maggie didn't want to risk anyone trying to harm them. She started up the sidewalk which was about seventy feet away from the back door. The faster she tried to walk balancing the two boys the more she kept slipping in the snow. The back door seemed to get farther and farther away. She kept looking over her shoulder watching for anyone that might come from behind. Maggie finally reached the back door fumbling for the house keys that she had shoved in her coat pocket. After getting through the back door safely with the boys, she quickly slammed and locked it behind them.

The boys were still half asleep when she got them upstairs and locked the second door. Maggie got them settled in their room and went to look out the window. There didn't seem to be anyone out there that she could see. Lee's bedroom faced the backyard so you could see the garage clearly. She had already gone to bed. When Lee awoke shewas startled when she saw Maggie standing in her room. "What are you doing looking out the window? Is something wrong?" Maggie was still shook up when she was telling Lee what happened as she constantly looked out the window. Lee calmly told her, "it's probably just your dad visiting you for the holidays." Not convinced, Maggie was still looking out the window when the lights went out. She yelled, "they went out." She stood there stunned still staring out the window. When she turned to say something to Lee, she was no longer in her bed. She was standing in the kitchen.

Maggie looked at her and said, "what is wrong with you? You were the one that told me that it was just my dad."

"I was fine until you told me that the lights went out." Lee stood there completely wide awake.

Maggie had refused to go back out there until the morning.

Once she was in the garage she looked around and nothing seemed out of place, the boys gifts were still in the back seat right where they had left them when she pulled both of them out of the car. She walked over to the light switch and turned it on. When she did, the lights went on, she flipped the switch off and they went out. To her surprise they worked perfectly fine.

Chapter 26

Maggie had decided to start fixing up the house, it had been in a state of disrepair for awhile. Her father had slowly let the place fall apart after her mother died. It was sad, because for an older home he had so much potential. One of the first things on the to do list was to replace the old fuse box down stair with a new breaker box. She also wanted to put a patio in the back yard, she had always enjoyed sitting outside. There was something about the smell of the summer air at night scented with apple blossoms and roses. Maggie had went to see her next store neighbor Don. He owned a construction business and hoped that he would be able to do the concrete work that she wanted to have done.

There was also an old cistern downstairs. It wasn't uncommon for a lot of the older homes in the neighborhood to have them. The purpose was for collecting rain water to use to do laundry, and for other household needs. The one that was downstairs was L shaped, and there was a three and a half foot wall that wrapped around. It was three feet by five and a half feet deep, the cement lid that coved it had broken over the years and was laying on the bottom in pieces. When Maggie was young she always felt uneasy when she walked by it. She still did even now. There was always that smell of damp earth. When you looked towards the center you could never really see the bottom. As a child she always imaged there were horrible creatures that lived in there. As an adult she would laugh and say, "maybe it's the portal to hell."

Maggie had the idea that since it had a three and a half foot wall around it she would have them fill it in with concrete and put folding doors the rest of the way up. It could be used as a storage area and hopefully that would also eliminate the odor that would rise up from the middle of it.

It was late spring and Don said that he would be able to get the patio poured, but he had asked her if she could wait on filling in the cistern. He had a job in the city and wanted to bring back pieces of concrete to fill the inside of the cistern. He told her that concrete was expensive and it would save her over five hundred dollars if she did it that way. Maggie liked the idea of saving money on that job because that meant that see could paint and wallpaper the boy's room.

Maggie had a set idea of what the perfect home was. She had that for a little while when her mother was alive. The living room was picture perfect. The smell of homemade pies and raisin bread filled the air. Maggie didn't know how her mother did it. She worked, she never drove so she took the train into the city. Her mother worked at Western Electric like most of her family did. She came home, cooked dinner, tended to two children, and was dying. Maggie's mother knew that she had cancer. The doctors advised her father not to tell her how bad it was, they felt that she should live out her life however she wanted. That's how it was in the sixties.

After her mother died her father started drinking from morning to night. He would pass out at the kitchen table until the morning. Sometimes he would go to work, and sometimes he would just start drinking all over again.

Things fell apart in the house, it came to the point that they only had one chair in the living room and a TV set. Maggie remembered when she got her first job, she bought a brand new living room set.

She didn't want the boys to feel ashamed of their home. She wanted them to have fond memories of where they grew up. She wanted that for them more them anything.

Chapter 27

It was Saturday and since Maggie didn't have to work, she mowed the lawn and decided to go to the nursery and pick up some rose bushes. She thought that they would go nicely along the side of the house. When she was growing up there were lilac bushes that lined the opposite side of the sidewalk, they grew over fifteen feet tall and arched over the walkway. When the kitchen window was open the house smelled heavenly. Through the years like everything around the house they were neglected and slowly died off.

It took most of the afternoon, but Maggie finally got everything planted. She just couldn't shake the feeling that someone was watching her. Maggie always felt uncomfortable being on that side of the house. She thought that maybe it had something to do with her childhood. When she was younger, her mother told her to put to put her bike away. It was dark out and she saw someone hiding behind the lilac bushes. When Maggie ran in the house and told her mother, whoever it was, was no longer there when her mother went outside.

Maggie reassured herself that there was no one else there. The boys occupied themselves playing in the backyard. She had build them a sandbox that they liked to play in with their Tonka trucks. Maggie was proud of herself. She was becoming quite handy around the house.

Maggie was ready to kick back and relax. She really felt that she had earned it after working in the yard all day. The boys had finally fallen asleep. She jumped in the shower and now it was what Maggie like to call her, "me time." It was about 9:30, so she turned on the TV and flopped down on the couch. Shortly after that, she heard the front porch screen door open followed by footsteps. Maggie didn't really think anything about it she just assumed that it was her brother Phil. Five minutes had pasted and he still hadn't come in yet, which she thought was strange. Still hearing the footsteps she looked out the window and no one was there. Maggie jumped up not quite sure what to do. She ran and locked the front door and yelled down the hall for Lee.

"What the hell are ya yelling about?" Lee said, "I'm not deaf."

"I was laying on the couch and I heard footsteps, ya know the ones Theresa was always talking about. I thought it was my brother but it wasn't." Just then they both heard the front porch door open and close . "Okay, maybe Theresa wasn't so crazy after all," Maggie admitted. It was getting to the point that neither one of them knew what to do. After all no one was being hurt, they were just noises. If they both tried hard enough they were sure that they could come up with a logical explanation. Maggie had dealt with hearing all sorts of strange noises in the house her whole life. She was always told that they were the usual house noises. It just seemed like now things were getting a little too real.

When Maggie went to bed that night she couldn't stop thinking about the footsteps that she heard on the front porch, or how the screen door opened and closed and no one was there. She started to drift off to sleep when she noticed a pressure pushing down on her, it felt like her whole body was being pulled down into the mattress. Maggie tried to sit up, but she was unable to move. It was almost like she was paralyzed. In her head she knew that she was awake because she was aware of the fact that she couldn't move. Maggie kept struggling to sit up, but she couldn't break free from whatever had her pinned to the bed. She started to fall asleep again when she awoke, because it felt like the air in her lungs was being squeezed out of her. Desperate to get up she started to jerk her hand back and forth, that was all she could manage to move. Then she was able to force her eyes wide open, but Maggie was still unable to get up when she drifted back to sleep, still feeling the numbness in her body. She fought again and was able to move her foot back and forth trying to make herself sit up. Finally with all her strength she forced herself into a sitting position before she completely stopped breathing. Maggie swung her legs over the edge of the bed, she stood up and walked into the living room. She needed to reassure herself that she wasn't paralyzed. Sitting on the couch she fell asleep in an upright position.

The following morning when she woke up Lee was standing in front of her, "are you okay? Why are you sleeping out here, sitting up?"

"Something happened last night....I was so scared." Maggie didn't even know how to explain it to Lee. They sat at the kitchen table drinking coffee as Maggie tried the best that she could to tell Lee what happened last night when she noticed the look on her face. "What is it? Your just staring at me like I'm insane."

"The same thing happened to me last week," Lee told her. I was afraid to say anything about it, to be real honest with you , it scared the shit out of me."

"You should have told me."

Over the next few weeks neither one of them had any problems sleeping, but they had decided that if it happened again they would see if it coincided with any of the noises or footsteps that they had been hearing.

Chapter 28

Don had started to work on filling in the cistern for Maggie. Don and one of his buddies Rich, started to put in the pieces of broken concrete that they got from the job they were working on in the city. Don was standing inside of the cistern and Rich was feeding him the rocks through a small window on the right side of the house. It was a slow process but they were making progress.

Don had lost his footing when something startled him. "What the hell are ya doing?" Rich asked.

"It felt like something just tried to grab my leg ."

"Quit being such a pussy and stop whining. I wanna get this shit done so we can hit the bar and have a couple of beers."

"Yah, you just wanna hit on that hot bartender," Don said.

"Oh hell yah," Rich bellowed. " She's got a hell of a rack."

They kept at it until they finished up about six o'clock.

"It's party time, let's hit it," Rich declared.

When Maggie got home that night she checked to see how far Don had gotten. She was pleased with his progress. Lorraine was asleep on the couch and Lee was at the kitchen table reading the Enquirer. "Really Lee," Maggie said.

"What? Mom bought it, you know she likes reading this crap."

"Yah, but that doesn't mean you have to read it," Maggie teased.

"Yah well, I was bored. What can I say."

Just then Maggie heard Luke coughing, he also sounded like he was gasping for air, she ran into his room and grabbed him. "What's wrong Sweetie? Tell me."

"There heavy," Luke said. "It's hard to breathe."

"What's heavy Sweetie?"

"The rocks," Luke said gasping.

By that time Lorraine woke up, "what's going on?"

"I think Luke's bronchitis is acting up. Can someone please run the shower. Make it hot, he needs the steam."

"I'll do it," Lee said.

Maggie sat in the bathroom with Luke rocking him back and forth for about an hour before his breathing returned to normal. Maggie was exhausted. She put Luke in her bed, if he had any other problems she would be right there by his side.

"What do you think he meant when he said the rocks are to heavy?" Lee asked.

"I don't know."

"I think there is something going on here Maggie. I think you know it too," Lorraine said. "I can help you with it."

"I know that you think you can.....and maybe you can, but right now I'm tired and I have to get up early for a parent teacher conference in the morning. I have to get some sleep. We can talk in the morning."

Maggie and Luke slept in. It was almost nine o'clock when they got up. It was a rough night, but Luke woke up feeling fine. He actually didn't seem to remember any of it. Maggie was relieved, because she didn't know exactly how she would ask him what he meant when he said that he couldn't breathe because the rocks were so heavy. Maggie poured herself a cup of coffee and sat down at the kitchen table.

"How's he feeling?" Lorraine asked.

"He doesn't seem to remember any of it," Maggie replied.

"I know you may not want to hear this but I think that there's something unnatural going on."

"You mean something supernatural?" Maggie said.

At that point Lee woke up and poured herself a cup of coffee. "I heard you guys talking. You know, maybe it wouldn't hurt to see if you could find out who lived here before your dad bought this house. That's what they always do in the movies," Lee suggested.

"Yah well, there was also a talking horse and a Jeannie that lived in a bottle on TV, this is real life. I'm afraid that it's affecting my kids," Maggie snapped. "I'm sorry, I know the both of you are just trying to help......maybe I'll try to see about looking into who lived here before my dad bought the place, but right now I need to get ready to go talk to Luke's teacher."

Maggie was Miss. Kinney's first parent of the day. Barbara Kinney was upbeat and energetic, she loved all her kids and they loved her too. "I wanted to let you know that Luke is a great student and very bright. I have talked with the principle and we both agree that he should attend summer school this year."

Maggie looked puzzled, "I thought that you just said that Luke was a very bright student?"

"I'm sorry if I confused you. We think that he is eligible for the gifted student program." All at once Maggie felt like she would burst. The smile on her face was huge. After the night she had, that made her feel a lot better. Maggie was proud of both of her son's.

"So here is some literature we want you to read. There would be a small fee for him to attend. We weren't sure what your financial situation was, I understand that your divorced."

Maggie cut in, "It doesn't matter, he will attend. I'll get the money."

All of a sudden Barbara's demeanor changed as she became very solemn.

"What is it?" Maggie asked.

"I don't usually ask personal questions, but is everything okay at home?"

"Why do you ask?"

"Because of this." Just then Barbara pulled out what looked like a drawing done in crayon. "Here," Barbara handed it to Maggie.

It appeared to be a picture of a sad little red haired girl. In the picture she was crying and holding herself between her legs.

"What is this?" Maggie asked.

"Do you have a daughter or any other children living with you?"

"No I don't, what are you implying?"

"I'm sorry, I'm not implying anything, when I asked Luke who she was, he said that she was his special friend. When I asked why she was so sad, he said because they keep hurting her."

Maggie looked stunned, "who are they?"

"I don't know, I was hoping that you did."

"Can I keep this? When the time is right , I want to talk to him about this."

"Sure, and please let us know if there is anything the school or I can do to help. Sometimes children of divorced parents, no matter how well adjusted they seem to be still can suffer some anxiety."

"Thank-you, I will keep you posted, and please let me know right away if he is still talking about this or drawing anymore pictures."

"We will, and it was a pleasure to meet you."

"You too."

Maggie walked home as fast as she could, the school was only two blocks from the house.

"So how did it go at the school?" Lee asked.

"First off, where's your mom?"

"She went uptown. She took the boys for ice cream, why?"

Maggie showed Lee the picture that Luke drew. Lee looked confused, "what is this?"

"Luke drew it. The teacher said that when she asked him who

she was, he said, it was his special friend. Then he said, they keep hurting her."

"Who are they?"

"I don't know."

"Look," Lee said. "I know you don't want to hear this, but my mom thinks she can help."

"Lee, I love and respect your mom, but I know what she means when she says she wants to help. She's talking about a séance. Lee, you do remember why she stopped having them? Don't you remember what your Uncle Jim tried to do? I just don't want to invite anything else into this house that may be worse than what may already be here. Please promise me you won't say anything to your mom about this. Promise me please."

"I promise."

Just then Lorraine walked in with the boys. "Mom, mom your home." They both shouted.

"Hey I heard that Grandma Lorraine took you two for ice cream."

"Yah, I had chocolate and Creed had strawberry. Did you talk to my teacher?"

"Yes I did and she had nothing but good things to say about you."

"Everything was okay? He's doing good then?" Lorraine asked.

"Yes, the teacher told me that they what to send him to summer school for gifted children."

"Way to go Luke," Lee said, as she gave him a hug.

"I'm glad," Lorraine said, looking at Maggie as if she knew she wasn't telling her everything.

Chapter 29

Maggie was suppose to work late, but at the last minute it was cancelled. The parts that they needed didn't come in. Allen suggested, "why don't we go to the Cattle Company down the street. We can get a pizza and have some beers. This may be the last time for awhile that we'll get sprung early."

"That sounds like a good idea," Maggie said.

Everyone else chimed in, "let's go, we're all in."

The debate over what to get on the pizzas was settled. Gary didn't like mushrooms, Maggie didn't like pepperonis, and of course no one liked anchovies. Everyone was half starved when they finally got their food.

Maggie was surprised when Allen pulled her aside and asked, "do you think your friend Lee would be interested in going out with me?"

"You really like her, don't you?"

"Yah, yah I do, there's something about her that I can't get out of my head. I don't know if she told you anything about what happened the night of your party or not."

Maggie cut in, "yah, actually she did. I asked her if she needed me to kick your ass."

Allen laughed, "I felt really bad about that. Ever since then I just can't stop thinking about her."

Maggie didn't want to be the one to have to break his heart but, "I'm sorry Allen, but she's with someone else. I didn't even know that she was interested in anyone until she told me how she felt about my cousin."

"Wow, well I guess it's my loss, I just hope he treats her good, or I'll have to kick his ass."

"I hope so too," Maggie agreed.

Maggie got home late that night. She got out of the car and noticed that the back door was wide open. "What the hell is going on?" Once she walked in, she smelled a strong musty odor of damp earth. Maggie also noticed what appeared to be small muddy footprints going up the stairs. When she looked around the corner towards the basement, she noticed what looked like a haze coming up from the center of the cistern.

Maggie tried the upstairs back door, when she turned the knob the door wouldn't open, it was locked. When Lee realized that Maggie was home she unlocked the door and pulled her in, "hurry up and get in here." Then she hurried and locked the back door again.

"What the hell is going on Lee? The downstairs back door was wide open."

"I was sound asleep when all of a sudden, it sounded like a car hit the side of the house. The boom was so loud it shook everything. When I got out of bed I heard what sounded like footsteps. It sounded like someone was coming up the back steps, so I ran and locked the back door. I grabbed the boys and put them in your room, and I'm not sure but it sounded like someone was turning the doorknob back and forth." Lee explained.

"Okay," Maggie said. "Enough is enough. We have to get down to the bottom of this and find out what is causing these noises. I don't know why, but I think that it has something to do with that damn cistern downstairs. Tomorrow I'm gonna go talk to Don and tell him to hold off on any more work in the basement."

Chapter 30

Maggie had gone next store to talk to Don. He invited her in for a cup of coffee. "So what's up?" Don asked.

She didn't know how to start, so she just came right out and said it, "Don I need you to stop working on the cistern."

"Hey, if you're not happy with the way things are going, I'm sure I can fix it," Don assured her.

"Don it's not that. You're not doing anything wrong."

"Then what is it? Something is bothering you?"

"Alright here goes. Your gonna think that I'm crazy but, I've always felt a little uneasy whenever I walked past that damn thing. I've been hearing noises, the last thing that happened was a couple of nights ago. There was a loud banging, footsteps, and muddy footprints. It's just that there has been a lot of weird shit going on lately and I can't help but think that it has something to do with that damn cistern."

Don just looked at her and said, "now can I tell you something? When Rich and I were putting the rocks in, I lost my balance be-cause.......well, it felt like something grabbed my leg. There I said it. I wanted to say something, but I was afraid that people would think that I had lost my damn mind." Don went on to say, "I want to show you something. I noticed these four small scratches on my leg, and there in the same spot where I thought something had grabbed my leg."

Maggie looked at him and shook her head and said, "either there is something very strange going on or we're both damn nuts."

Don called Rich and told him what they needed to do. Maggie could hear Rich say from where she was sitting, "are you fucking kidding me Don? Do you know how hard it was to put all that shit in there, and now you want to fucking take it all back out?"

"Look man, I know it was a lot of work and I can't really explain it right now, but it needs to be done, and it's not like you're doing it for free. I am paying you." Don said to Rich.

Chapter 31

First thing Monday morning Don and Rich started taking out the pieces of concrete rock that they put in the cistern a week before. As they started to reach the bottom Don noticed something strange in the corner. "It looks like a toy," Don said. "This wasn't here earlier."

Maggie asked, "what is it ......what did you find?" He handed it to her, Maggie was stunned. It was Creed's transform grimlock. That just sent chills through her, "keep going, see if you can find anything else," Maggie said.

"Looks like someone had tried to dig farther down in the corner," Don said. "It's been covered with broken pieces of the original lid to the cistern."

Don probed a little farther down and he found an old Chinese checkers board with a few marbles thrown about. Then he came across an old ceramic kitten. When he held it up Maggie shouted, "oh my God, let me see that."

He handed it to her. "Does that mean something to you?" Don asked.

"This was mine. My mother gave this to me when I was a little girl. She knew I always loved cats. I wrote the name Mittens on the bottom of it. Then one day it just disappeared. I blamed my brother for taking it, things would always go missing and we blamed each other for it . How the hell did it get down here? Can you keep look-ing?" Maggie asked.

All of a sudden Don abruptly stopped, he couldn't move.

"What is it?" Maggie asked.

"It looks like an old army duffle bag."

"Can you see what's in it?"

"No, but maybe you should call the police."

"Why?"

"Unless there's some kind of doll in the bag it looks like the out-line of.....just call the police."

Maggie called the police, and the three of them waited outside for them to arrive. The two officers that answered the call were the same two that were sent whenever Theresa would call. Which ex-plained Officers Coswell and Henley's sarcastic attitude.

"All right where is this so called duffle bag that is buried in your basement?"

Maggie wanted so badly to make a smart ass comment, but in-stead she bit her lip.

Don walked over to the officer and said, "I'm the one that found it, and it's over there in the corner. You'll have to use that step latter to climb up in there."

Once Officer Coswell was inside, Don stepped back. Coswell examined the bag and found the opening. He then slowly opened the bag and looked inside. Coswell looked at both Don and Maggie, "you wasted our time by calling us down here to look in an empty bag?"

Don and Maggie looked at each other shocked. Don thought for sure that they would find something in there. "Are you sure that it's empty?" Maggie asked.

Coswell picked up the bag to show them. He stumbled back and fell. The color in his face had completely drained, he was white as a ghost. Maggie followed his eyes to see what he was staring at, and what she saw made her sick to her stomach. Clutching the end of the bag was a small hand and part of an arm that was decayed.

Once Coswell pulled himself together he told his partner Henley, "we need to call the county and get a forensics team out here." Coswell then apologized to Don and Maggie for his attitude.

"Look, I know that Theresa called you out here a lot of times. I also know that you were never able to find anything. That's why I never called when we started hearing noises, but just because you can't always explain something doesn't mean that there isn't something going on." Maggie said.

Chapter 32

The one good thing was that the boys were in school, so they didn't have to witness any of this. When Maggie picked them up she told them that they were going on an adventure. They were going to spend the night in a hotel, and the one that they were going to even had a swimming pool. She had hoped that the forensics team wouldn't take long to collect whatever they needed to get out of basement. As it turned out, they were able to remove the remains that night. They came back the following day to finish up.

The case was handed over to the DuPage County homicide detectives division. It was assigned to Detective's Branch and Logan. Erich Branch was young, he made detective when he was thirty one. He was an outstanding police officer that moved up through the ranks quickly and was well respected by his superiors. John Logan had been on the force for about twenty five years, he was a well seasoned detective that didn't pull any punches. He definitely didn't take any shit from anyone. At first glance the two seemed like a mismatched pair, but they actually complimented each other and worked well together.

The medical examiner, Dr. Judith Kirkland was a middle aged women that looked like she had seen better days. She probably hadn't smiled since she took the job in the medical examiner's office, but then again who could blame her. Judith had seen more than her share of atrocities.

Branch and Logan paid Dr. Kirkland a visit. They were looking for information, anything that might help them to identify the remains.

"I've determined that the remains were of a little girl in the age range of eight or nine years old," Dr. Kirkland said. "Also, judging by the condition of the teeth, I would say that she's been there at least forty or fifty years."

"Do you mean she's never been to a dentist?" Logan asked.

"No that's not what I mean, they didn't start putting fluoride in the water until 1945, her teeth show signs of decay due to a lack of fluoride. I also estimate that her clothes date back at least that far," Kirkland said.

"Do you know how she died?" Branch asked.

"I can tell you this, she didn't have an easy life. There were sign of old fractures that did not heal properly. So I would guess that she's never seen a doctor for those injuries. Her pelvic bone was broken and I believe that happened right before she died. She may have also had a head injury, but I don't think it would have killed her, although it may have rendered her unconscious." Kirkland hesitated, she was trying to pull herself together.

" What is it ?" Logan asked.

" I think she may have been alive when she was buried."

"What makes you say that?" Branch asked.

"She had what they call a death grip on the duffle bag that was on top of her. If she was unconscious, whoever did this to her may have thought she was dead and placed her in that hole and buried her. At some point and time she may have regained consciousness, then struggled to get out by pulling on the bag, but because of her injuries it may have to painful for her to crawl out. This little girl suffered her whole life at the hands of some sick bastard. You need to find out who she is and who did this to her. No one deserves to die like that."

Chapter 33

Both Detectives knew that they could rule out Maggie as being a suspect. She wasn't even born forty years ago. They also knew that they could rule out her parents as having anything to do with it, they didn't live in the house back then.

The Detectives went back to Maggie's house. They let her know what they had learned from the M.E about the remains that were found in the basement. Maggie was in shock, she couldn't believe that she had lived there all her life with a body that had been buried in her home.

"Do you believe in ghosts?" Maggie asked the Detectives.

"Not really," Logan said. "Why?"

"When I was growing up, I remember as a little girl, I would always hear these noises. Sometimes it would sound like there was someone locked in my closet, just turning the door knob back and forth. I would hear click, click, click. My dad would say, oh that's just the furnace turning on. I knew that wasn't right, the sound was coming from my closet. There were also the voices I would hear late at night. My parents would always say that it was coming from baseball field, but that field was more than four blocks away. I think the one that perplexes me the most is, sometimes I would hear what sounded like marbles falling. You know that they found some marbles that went to an old Chinese checkers game in that hole she was buried in?"

"We know, they also found some other toys that belonged to you and your son," Branch said.

"How do you explain that?" Maggie asked.

"We can't," Logan told her. "We do need to ask you some questions."

"What kind if questions? You can't possibly think I had anything to do with this?"

"No, we know you and your family didn't have anything to do with this. What we would like to know is if you might have an idea of who your parents may have bought this house from?"

"Oh God, I would have no way of knowing that," Maggie said. "I was just a baby when we moved here. There are still a couple of old timers that live on the block.

They may be able to tell you more then I can. Mr. Donavon lives two houses down, and Gracie lives across the street in the yellow house."

Branch and Logan went to talk to Frank Donovan first. When they knocked on his door they were greeted by a balding man in his eighties who made it seem as if it was a big imposition to even answer the door. "What is it?" He snarled.

"I'm Detective Logan and this is Detective Branch."

"Yah so, state you business."

"We're here to ask you some questions."

"Bout what?"

"We weren't sure if you had heard, but there were some remains found in the basement of the house two doors down. We would like to know if you knew the family that lived there prior the Stanczyk family."

"I don't know anything, and I ain't got the time for this." Frank Donovan slammed the door in the detectives' face.

"I don't think we'll be getting any information out him," Logan said sarcastically.

They hoped that they would have better luck with Grace Gerlando. Grace was well into her sixties with dark hair and more energy than most thirty year olds. She knew a lot about the people and the neighborhood, not because she was nosey, but because she enjoyed talking to people. Most of the kids on the block loved to play with her cats, Smokey and BoBo kitty.

"I really didn't know Mr. Androvich, by the time I moved in the neighborhood he was the only on living in the house. He really didn't speak to anyone that I ever saw. He just always seemed to be a very angry man," Grace said.

"He never spoke to anyone?" Logan questioned.

"Well I did see him talking to Frank Donovan, and I also saw him talk to Edward Remic. Actually the three of them always acted very secretive, but you know who may know something, Estelle, she was Edward Remic's daughter. They lived in the corner house, and she may have been around the same age as that little girl you found."

"Do you know where we can find her?" Branch asked.

"She lives in a retirement home in Milwaukee now. I still get a Christmas card from her. Let me see if I can find it, I believe that there is a return address on the envelope."

Chapter 34

Monday morning Branch and Logan left for Milwaukee, it was an hour and a half drive. They decided to stop at the first restaurant they came across, they knew it was going to be a long day.

When they got to Bending Willows Retirement home, Estelle was already waiting for them, "Gracie told me that you might come."

Estelle was a mousey looking women in her early seventies. "Sad thing about Emma Rose."

"You know who she is?" Logan asked.

"Who else could it be? I knew her daddy had to of done something to her. He didn't like that child, he didn't much like anyone. My daddy was kinda like that too."

"Why don't you just start from the beginning." Branch said, pulling out his notepad.

"Who owned that house?" Logan asked.

"Their names were George and Ester Androvich. Ester would talk to my mama every now and then, mainly when he wasn't around. He didn't like anyone around his family. I remembered that she was such a nice lady. I know that my mama asked her once why he was so mean. She told her that he didn't really mean to be that way, she said that he was from Czechoslovakia and when he was a little boy his parents made him sleep in the barn. They would feed him the scraps off the dinner table after they were done eating. Why would you do that to a child? I guess that was one of the reasons he was the way he was......who knows what else they may have done to him. Anyway, Ester came over one day, she was frantic. She told my mama that she was on her way to the market when she realized she forgot her change purse......well, when she got back to the house she heard Emma crying. That bastard locked her in the closet, she was holding herself, you know, down there. I think he touched her. Ester tried never to leave Emma Rose alone with him again."

"Why didn't Ester leave him?" Branch asked.

"You don't understand, you didn't dare do that, not back then. A women was expected to get married, have babies and obey their husband. Divorce was a sin against God and the church, but I think that there should be a special place in hell for anyone that hurts a child."

Estelle went on to say, "I think he knew Ester was on to him. She knew what he was doing to that little girl, that's why I think he killed her."

"He killed his wife?" Logan asked.

"Well that's what I think. He called it an accident, said she fell down the back steps carrying a laundry basket. Must of lost her footing, he said. She broke her neck. I think he pushed her."

"What happened to Emma Rose?"

"She went to go live with her gramma. I knew that she would be okay, her gramma loved that little girl. She bought her some toys. She'd never had any, bought her a real pretty doll and this Chinese checkers game they would play together all the time. Then her gramma had a heart attack and died."

"What happened to Emma then?"

"She had to go back home and live with her daddy. I used to see her sitting on the front porch, she looked so alone. I was a few years older than her, so I would go over and talk to her. She shouldn't have, but she asked me to come in. I think she was so starved for attention that, I don't think she cared if her daddy was gonna be mad at her for doing it. She just wanted me to play checkers with her, she loved that game and she just wanted a friend."

"What happened next?" Branch asked.

"Her daddy came home and when he saw that she let a stranger in he was so mad, the look in his eyes......he looked like a monster. He grabbed Emma Rose and started hitting her. He threw that game against the wall, marbles went everywhere. I ran home as fast as I could. I locked myself in my room, I was so scared that he was gonna come after me next. I had nightmares after that, for a long time."

"Did you tell anyone what happened?"

"I know I should have, but I was so afraid that he would do something to me. I finally saw Emma Rose a couple of days later. She had bruises all over her."

Estelle started to cry, "I can't help but think that if I would have said something to someone....that Emma Rose would still be alive."

"What happened after that?"

"I never saw Emma Rose after that, George told my daddy he didn't have no time to bother with no kid, so he said he signed some papers and let the county take her. Let her be someone else's problem, that's what he called her, a problem."

"I always thought that my daddy knew more than he was sayin. When my mama would ask what he was talking to George about, he would always say that was none of her business, that it was between us men, he'd say."

"Do you know what happened to George?"

"I heard that he had some kinda accident at work. I know that he worked in some machine shop in Chicago and he got caught in his press, they said he was crushed to death. I know it's wrong, but I can't say that I was sorry to hear that. The county couldn't find any other relatives, so they took the house and sold it to that other family."

"After I moved away I would come and visit my mama from time to time, I would see that little girl, I think her name was Maggie, she reminded me so much of Emma Rose. Same red hair and freckles, she also had that same sad look. I think her mama died too, cancer I think. I just hoped that nothing bad was happening to her."

"Thank-you, you've been very helpful Mrs. ...."

"Oh, it's Miss. I've never been married. I guess I didn't want to wind up like my mama."

"You know..... my parents were married almost sixty years and in the end they found my mama laying on the kitchen floor. She had a stroke, and my daddy just kept tending to his damn lawn. Finally after four days the police checked in on them and found her, if he just would have gotten her the help she needed, they said she would have survived."

"We are sorry, Miss. Remic."

"I'm glad you found that little girl, maybe she can finally rest in peace now. It's just always haunted me, not knowing what really happened to her."

"I don't think that you're the only one that was haunted by this." Branch said.

Part 6

From Out of the Darkness
and Into the Light

Chapter 35

Logan and Branch didn't get back until six that evening. "I think we should call it a day," Branch suggested.

"I agree, I think tomorrow's gonna be another long day," Logan said. "We need to talk to the M.E and let her know what Estelle Remic told us, see if what she said fits with what Kirkland has determined about the remains. Then we need to see Maggie Jacobs and tell her who the remains belong to."

Tuesday Branch and Logan went to the M.E's office to talk to Kirkland. They told her about their visit with Estelle. "Well that would be consistent with some of the injuries I found on the remains," Kirkland said. "I feel confident in saying the remains that were found belong to Emma Rose Androvich."

Maggie was getting ready to go to the grocery store when Logan rang the door bell. She invited them in, "I just made fresh coffee, can I get you a cup?"

"We wanted to let you know that we have identified the remains," Branch informed her.

"Who is she?"

"Her name was Emma Rose. Her parents owned this house before your family bought it."

"Who killed her?" Maggie dreaded finding out the answer to that question.

"The best that we can determine, from the information that we gathered is that it was her father. We were told that he abused her. There also may have been others involved."

"What do you mean others.......like other neighbors?"

"We're not sure. We may never know the answer to that, but we do know that her father was definitely involved. He may have even killed her mother."

"Oh my God, that poor little girl. No one deserves that."

Maggie couldn't help but think that in some ways her and Emma Rose's life were similar. She had also thought that would explain some of the noises she heard when she was a child. Could it have been Emma Rose wanting someone to find her, and free her from the hell she was trapped in.

Maggie asked the Detectives what was going to happen to the remains. They told her that she would probably be buried in a paupers grave. She had no other family that they knew of, so there would be no one to claim her remains.

"Look, I have an uncle that owns the funeral home in town. Let me talk to him and see if maybe he can help."

"I don't see a problem with it," Branch said.

Maggie went to see her Uncle Paul. She told him everything that had happened, although by that time the whole town knew about the remains of Emma Rose. What had surprised Maggie was that a lot of the towns people had tried to enquire about doing something for Emma. A lot of people wanted her to have a decent burial.

"Do you think that you might be able to find out where her mother and grandmother are buried?"

"I'll be real honest with you, it could take some time. The county didn't keep very good records back then, and without knowing if they were buried in this area or somewhere else, that could make it difficult to find them. I promise you I will try."

"I understand that, she's waited this long. I don't think a little longer would hurt."

Maggie, Lee, and Lorraine were sitting at the table having their coffee when Lee said, "have you noticed that the noises have stopped?"

"I think that you were right Maggie. Emma Rose just wanted someone to hear her so she could be found," Lorraine said.

"I've talked to the teacher and she told me that Luke hasn't talked about his special friend anymore. He hasn't drawn anymore pictures either, as a matter of fact she told me that he has really excelled in his summer school program."

"I think that this is finally over."

Just then Maggie heard a knock on the front door. It was her Uncle Paul. "Hey come on in," Maggie said.

"I'm so sorry it took so long. I know it's been a few months, and it wasn't easy to find Emma's family."

"But you did find them?"

"Yes I did, actually they are in a old cemetery about fifteen miles from here. It's not used anymore, some of the residents buried there date back to the earlier 1800's. It's still kept up, but no one really goes to visit anymore."

"Can she still be buried there with her family?"

"Yes, I talked to the appropriate people and they agreed it would be the right thing to do."

October 15th 1987 was a beautiful autumn day. Along with Maggie, Lee, and Lorraine, were Gracie Gerlando and Estelle Remic. Walking over to the small casket that held the remains of Emma Rose, Estelle touched it. "I am so sorry that I never did anything to help you. I was so scared, I was afraid to say anything. I can't imagine all the horrible things that you went through," Estelle said crying. "May you finally find the peace that you deserve."

Nearly fifty years after her death, Emma Rose was laid to rest next to the two people that loved her the most in life.

Author's Note

Monsters are real, and ghosts are real too. They live inside us, and sometimes they win.

STEPHEN KING, attributed, *A Book of Horrors*

━━●(◉)●━━

The contents of this book are loosely based on true events that have happened to the individuals in this book. The footsteps, the lights that went on a off, along with the banging noises, doors opening and closing, and séances were all actual events. Emma Rose is a fictional character that the author created to give an explanation to some of the noises and other events that occurred. It is human nature to want closure or a logical explanation to the unknown. The truth is that sometimes there is no logical explanation for the things that go bump in the night.

About the Author

C.T Huguelet grew up in the small town of Westmont in Illinois, and to this day still has fond memories of living there. She enjoys spending time with her family and grandchildren. The love of her life is a pilot and owns his own plane, they've spent many hours down through the years flying together. She has a passion for horror movies as well as mystery and true crime novels. Now she has decided to follow her dream, to write a book of her own.

CPSIA information can be obtained
at www.ICGtesting.com
Printed in the USA
LVHW031323020721
691743LV00002B/166